To prevent her making an unsuitable marriage, Claire's father had tricked her into going out to Tanzania—out of mischief, he had supposed. But it all led to her falling in love with Rod Gilvray, a man who was not of her world and who regarded her as equally unsuited to be his wife. Just what had her father achieved by his interference?

NO PASSING FANCY

BY

KAY THORPE

MILLS & BOON LIMITED
15–16 BROOK'S MEWS
LONDON W1A 1DR

First published 1980
Australian copyright 1980
Philippine copyright 1980
This edition 1980

© Kay Thorpe 1980

ISBN 0 263 73363 7

Set in Linotype Plantin 10 on 11½ pt.

Made and printed in Great Britain by
Richard Clay (The Chaucer Press), Ltd., Bungay, Suffolk

CHAPTER ONE

THE Rolls came smoothly up the curving drive and drew to a halt at the foot of the broad flight of stone steps leading to the front door. Watching from the vantage point of her bedroom window, Claire could see two people seated in the rear of the car. That meant Bill had brought home a weekend guest. She wondered idly if it was anyone she knew. Not that it made any great difference. His business acquaintances were all much of a muchness, hardly what you might call scintillating company at the very best.

Regardless, she stayed where she was as the chauffeur nipped smartly out of his seat to open the rear door and let the two passengers out. First the familiar thickset figure of her father, balding head gleaming in the early evening sunlight, followed by a younger man dressed in a casual suede jacket and light slacks whose thick crop of hair looked the colour of teak seen from above. Foreshortened as he was by the angle of her viewing, she judged him around the six foot mark, and well built with it. The rugged, outdoor type, she thought dryly, catching a glimpse of square-jawed features as he lifted his head to look at the house. Different from the usual run perhaps, yet still unlikely to add any zest to the weekend. He looked distinctly lacking in the lighthearted fun department.

His voice was good, though, carrying up to her as he commented on the appearance of the building in front of him: deep-timbred and masculine. Educated, but not public school, Claire decided, mentally comparing it with that of Peter St John which most decidedly was. Rather a pity she hadn't followed her initial instincts earlier and invited Peter over to dinner. It might have been interesting comparing two such opposing types.

She pulled the casement fully closed as the two men disappeared into the house, turning back to look at her familiar, luxurious bedroom with a faint sigh. Over an hour until dinner and nothing to do except change. It promised to be a long dull evening. For a moment she contemplated phoning Peter and asking him to take her out somewhere to dinner, but it was only for a moment. It was a little too late to start changing her plans now. Her father would have been told she was home and would be expecting her at their own table to help entertain his guest, whoever the latter was. Still, at least he was someone new to impress. Her interest perked up a little at the thought. It had been some time since she had made any fresh conquests, moving always with the same crowd the way she did. Perhaps this man her father had brought home might provide some divertissement from boredom, if only for a short time.

She really should do something about finding herself a job of some kind, Claire acknowledged ruefully, opening one of the wardrobes which lined the whole of one wall of the room. But doing what? At twenty-two, with both school and art college behind her, she still had little notion of what she wanted. Textile design had been her original aim, but the competition had been too fierce and the incentive too weak for more than a halfhearted stab. For her it would have been a hobby rather than a livelihood, so why even attempt to oust others for whom an independent income was essential?

Marriage could be one solution, she supposed. Peter seemed keen enough on the idea. Except that she had a feeling she might simply be exchanging one form of boredom for another. She and Peter got along wonderfully well as friends and lighthearted companions, but could she really see herself living with him? They were too much alike in many ways. No stability. Yet perhaps marriage itself would bring forth that quality in them both.

She had been gazing for several moments at the row of garments without seeing them. Now she brought her mind into focus and selected a calf-length burgundy silk she knew made her dark hair even darker and fitted her like a glove. Had she and Bill been dining alone she wouldn't have bothered to dress up at all, but impressions were not made in casual clothes.

Quite when she had first begun calling her father by his first name, Claire could scarcely remember. It came far more naturally to her than Daddy or Father. He himself had never objected, and seemed unperturbed by the attitude of those of their visitors who patently disapproved of the habit. Most people were accustomed to it by now and had stopped registering any kind of reaction. No doubt they had long since put the whole thing down to her lack of a mother to teach her elementary respect.

Claire's mother had died a few hours after her birth, leaving her to spend her formative years in the care of an over-indulgent maiden aunt while her father had been busy building up the business which still occupied the greater part of his time. The name Naughton was synonymous these days with some of the finest engineering constructions in both hemispheres, a reputation he had acquired by employing only the best both in men and materials. Ten years ago he had bought this house standing in five acres of grounds only forty miles from his office in town, but he was all too rarely in it. Whatever money could buy was Claire's for the asking, and often not even that, as she had a very generous allowance of her own. If sometimes she felt she would have given the lot to be part of a real family she kept such thoughts strictly private. Better to be rich than poor in any circumstances, she told herself stoutly on such occasions.

Showered and dressed, she made her way down the imposing staircase some time later, exchanging a smile with the new maid, Louise, who was crossing the hall. It was nice to have someone closer to her own age group around the house, although Alice had always been pleasant enough. They'd been lucky to find a replacement so soon after the other's retirement, especially as Louise was fairly local and therefore able to visit her family often. She seemed to have settled in well enough, thank heaven. Keeping staff was almost as difficult as finding them these days. The few still willing to go into service could pick and choose, and they knew it.

The clink of glasses overlaid by the sound of her father's gruff accents came from the direction of the drawing room via the partially opened door. The man seated on the long sofa set at right angles to the fireplace came to his feet on Claire's entry, his glance moving over her in an appraisal which somehow prickled the hairs in the nape of her neck. He was even taller than she had first thought, his shoulders broad beneath the dark blue jacket. Steel grey in colour, his eyes registered a fleeting surprise.

Bill Naughton was watching his guest's reaction with a grin on his face. 'Not exactly a chip off the old block, is she?' he remarked, restopping the whisky decanter. 'Takes after her mother for looks, fortunately. Claire, this is Rod Gilvray.'

Green eyes widened with slow deliberation. '*The* Rod Gilvray?'

An eyebrow lifted faintly. 'There could be others.'

'Not in your line, I'm sure.' She was smiling, her tone light. 'Did Bill finally manage to get you on his payroll?'

'Finally.' There was satisfaction in her father's voice. 'He's taking over the Tanzanian job for starters. Drink?'

'Gin and tonic, please.' She went over as he poured it for her, taking the glass and turning back to look at the other man with bland enquiry. 'Bridging, isn't it? I'm surprised the Tanzanians can afford it.'

Behind her, Bill laughed. 'Stop playing the dumb female! The mining company is doing most of the paying, as you well know. With a hundred miles or more cut off the route they can have those phosphates rolling to the coast in double quick time and cover the cost inside a year. Open up the area too. There's scope for agricultural development, given better access.'

Claire held up her glass, mouth tilting. 'Here's to Third World philanthropy!'

Rod Gilvray made no move to raise his own glass in reply, studying her coolly as she drank. He sat down again when she moved to a chair, crossing one leg over the other with a casual air which was not lost on her.

'Your father tells me you're responsible for the decorations in here,' he said. 'Congratulations. It's beautifully done.'

'Planned, not executed,' she came back on a drawled note, and saw the corner of the strong mouth turn downwards.

'Naturally. I don't really see you on a ladder with a paintbrush in hand. There has to be a planner to tell the workers what to do, otherwise they'd spend most of their time running around in ever decreasing circles.'

Bill was looking from one to the other in obvious enjoyment. 'I think you might have met your match in this one,' he said to his daughter. 'About time somebody put you down a little!'

Claire smiled at him, not in the least disturbed. 'Down but not out, darling. Do I take it you'll be spending some time in West Africa yourself?'

'Some. Rod leaves on Monday. I'll take a trip out towards the end of the month. I gathered you've worked with the resident engineer before, Rod? That should make things considerably easier.'

'Not noticeably,' came the dry rejoinder. 'We don't always see eye to eye.'

'Oh well, as project manager, you can always spit in his if necessary,' Claire put in blandly. 'Yours is the overall control, after all.'

'Only so far as carrying out the agreed programme is concerned.' His tone was pleasant enough, but there was a definite glint in the grey eyes. 'Obviously you don't have too much understanding of the business.'

'In other words, keep your mouth closed if you don't know what you're talking about,' Bill chuckled. 'You're a brave man, Rod !'

Claire kept back her own retort with an effort, retaining her smile with an even greater one. This man needed cutting down to size, but words weren't going to do it. There were other ways—and a whole weekend in which to employ them. Suddenly the prospect seemed brighter.

'You're right,' she said. 'I was just talking for the sake of it. You'll have to tell me something about your job while you're here. I'd be interested to learn.'

He looked back at her steadily. 'Your father could tell you anything you want to know.'

'He isn't often around to ask.'

'True, I'm afraid,' Bill agreed on a rueful note. 'The price one pays.'

If any price had been paid it had been by her, not him, Claire thought in swift repudiation. He had been doing something he wanted to do, something which had meant more to him than she did—and still did mean more. If she had been a boy perhaps things might have been different; a son could have joined him in his interests. She became aware that Rod was still watching her, and quickly blanked off all expression from her face. Her relationship with her father was her own private concern and no one else's. She was relieved when Louise came in to announce that dinner was ready to be served.

During the meal she made a point of drawing out their guest to talk about himself, although she didn't learn a great deal. All she managed to gather was that he was not married, that he was somewhere in his early thirties and that he had no settled home owing to the demands of his job.

With regard to his outside interests he was a fraction more forthcoming, revealing a liking for music and theatre, when he had opportunity to indulge the latter, and a love of the martial arts which had brought him a black belt in judo.

Long-term constructional sites always incorporated re-creational facilities, he explained when Claire asked where and how he had found the time to develop that amount of skill. Judo had proved a winner with the men on more than one occasion, providing both mental and physical exercise of a different kind from that they were accustomed to practising during the course of a working day.

'It's a useful knowledge for women to have to hand in this day and age,' he added. 'It mightn't make walking around alone after dark any more advisable, but at least it provides a source of protection should the occasion ever arise. Given even a rudimentary training, a woman can quite feasibly throw a man twice her size.'

Claire looked him straight in the eye. 'You mean I could even throw you?'

His smile held a dry quality. 'It's possible but not likely. I was talking about a man who wouldn't be expecting it.'

'And you always would.'

'Let's say it becomes instinctive.'

'Oh yes,' she said softly. 'Let's.'

Bill coughed into the sudden little silence. 'We'll take the brandy with us into the study, Rod,' he said. 'I want to go all the way through the specification with you before you leave on Sunday. Tell Louise we'll have coffee in there too, will you, Claire.'

She made a sound of protest. 'You can't leave me to entertain myself for the whole evening!'

'I'm afraid we have to,' he returned firmly. 'I'm surprised you don't have any arrangements of your own tonight. You usually do.'

'Well, I don't.'

'It isn't too late to make some. Why don't you give young St John a ring? He'd be over like a flash if I know anything about him.'

Claire's head lifted, the presence of a third person forgotten for a moment. 'You don't know anything about him. You've barely spoken to him more than a dozen times.'

'What is there to say? We hardly have interests in common.'

'Just because he doesn't half kill himself with work the way you do it doesn't mean ...'

'Doesn't mean he's an idle layabout with more money than he knows what to do with? It's a matter of opinion. I blame his family. They should make him earn his living.'

'The way you had to.'

'Had was the operative word in my case. In his it would at least be character building.'

'I like his character the way it is,' Claire declared.

'Weak and willing?'

'That's a matter of opinion too.'

Bill Naughton caught his guest's eye and gave vent to a sudden sigh. 'Sorry about this, Rod. Shouldn't be airing family differences in front of you. You might have gathered my daughter has a mind of her own.'

'Like her father before her,' Rod responded with no

apparent sign of discomfiture, and drew a short laugh.

'Maybe so. We sure as hell don't share the same views on many things!'

'On *anything*,' Claire put in, tightlipped. She pushed back her chair with an abrupt movement and got to her feet. 'I'll take your advice this time, though. Expect me when you see me. Oh, and do enjoy your man-to-man, both of you!'

She made the call from the privacy of her room, glad to hear Peter's familiar tones on the other end of the line.

'I find myself at a loose end,' she said on a deliberately flippant note. 'How would you like to take me away from it all?'

'Where do you fancy?' he asked, playing up to her. 'The moon's full. We can't miss it if we aim straight.'

'Too far,' she said. 'I'll settle for a drive by the light of. Meet me at the gates in half an hour.'

He asked no questions. That was one of the things she liked about Peter St John. She changed quickly into slacks and a sweater, leaving her hair loose to her shoulders in the way he liked. It was too warm for a jacket, and she hardly needed a purse. She went downstairs with an air of insouciance, but the study door was fast closed and no sound came forth. Damn them both! she thought as she left the house.

The Lotus reached the main gates almost at the same moment she did, drawing to a smooth stop alongside her slenderly curved figure. Claire opened the near door and got in, sliding down into the seat with a casual familiarity, her glance going sideways to meet that of her rescuer.

'I didn't really expect to find you in tonight.'

The boyish good-looking face creased into a grin. 'I very nearly wasn't. Another fifteen minutes and you'd have missed me. Bill not come home?'

'He came.' Her tone was short. 'Let's drive out to the common. And for heaven's sake take it easy. One more endorsement and you lose your licence.'

'If that happens you'll have to do the driving instead,' he said unperturbed. He revved the engine before letting in the clutch, verifying the maker's claim of nought to sixty in nine seconds for the umpteenth time, then slowing for the bend in a way which made seat belts an absolute necessity. Claire made no further protest, aware that it would fall on deaf ears. For Peter, driving was all or nothing. What was the use, he would ask, of having a ton or more on the clock if one had to stick to a speed limit? Unfortunately the police didn't agree with that particular line of reasoning. Claire couldn't say she blamed them. Perhaps it would do Peter good to lose his licence for a period. Even slow wheels were better than no wheels at all.

They parked in a favourite spot overlooking the old quarry, but she pushed him away when he attempted to take her in his arms.

'I'm not in the mood,' she said. 'Do you have a cigarette?'

He gave her one a little sulkily, and took one for himself, smoking it in silence for a few minutes. 'I don't always understand you,' he said at length on an accusing note. 'Why did you ask me to bring you up here?'

Right at that moment, Claire didn't understand herself all that well. She felt on edge, wanting Peter to kiss her yet not wanting it too. Tonight for some reason his fair good looks failed to stir her. He was three years older than her, yet he seemed suddenly so much younger.

'I'm sorry,' she said. 'I had a row with Bill tonight.'

He glanced at her swiftly, expression altering. 'Over me?'

It was her turn to glance his way. 'What makes you think that?'

'He doesn't like me,' with a shrug. 'He's made that fairly

obvious. I don't suppose we have a lot in common.'

'No,' Claire agreed. 'He thinks you should have a regular job.'

'What does he call three company directorships?'

'A name on paper in your case,' she returned candidly. 'You don't actually do anything, do you?'

'Now and then.' His grin was appealing. 'Enough to merit the salaries I'm paid. Thanks to Grandmother, I don't need any more. I could even keep a wife.'

'And a family?'

'Ah, now that might be a different proposition. Still, cross bridges when you come to them, has always been my maxim.'

'I know.' She said it gently. 'It isn't one I'm sure I could live with, though.'

'How do you know till you've tried it? We could have a lot of fun, Claire. Marriage should be fun—at least in its initial stages.' Peter laid a tentative finger along the side of her face, moving it further down to trace the line of her mouth when she made no move to resist. 'We make an awfully attractive pair, darling.'

'Modesty not being your strong suit,' she came back, striving for a light note. 'You know, I suddenly feel like dancing. Let's go and find a disco. There's usually one in the village Friday nights.'

But there wasn't this particular Friday night. In the end they ran right into Romford before they found what they were looking for in the way of entertainment. It was gone one-thirty when they finally made it back. Peter drove her right to the door, getting out of the car to walk her up the steps.

'Do you have a key?' he asked. 'Seems they're all abed.'

Claire shook her head without particular concern. 'I didn't bring a purse.'

'So we'll have to ring the bell.' His arm was around her,

turning her towards him, his face laughing in the moonlight. 'But first ...'

He was still kissing her when the door opened. Startled, Claire turned her head to see Rod Gilvray framed in the doorway. He was wearing a dark silk dressing gown over paler pyjamas and looked entirely at home.

'Sorry,' he said without a trace of embarrassment. 'I heard the car and thought you might be having difficulty finding your key. Had a good evening?'

'Very.' Claire moved abruptly away from Peter. 'This is one of Bill's new employees. Rod Gilvray—Peter St John. You didn't have to come down.'

'I was already down.' He proffered no further explanation. Neither man had made any attempt to shake hands, acknowledging the introduction with brief nods of the head. 'I'll leave the door unlatched, if you like.'

'I'm coming in,' she said. 'I'll phone you tomorrow, Peter.'

The latter accepted his dismissal with obvious reluctance. Only after the door had closed between them did she hear him go back down the steps to the waiting car. The roar of the supercharged engine sounded devastatingly loud even from indoors.

Rod stood looking at her for a moment without speaking, expression difficult to define. Claire looked steadily back at him, waiting.

'I was having a drink,' he said. 'Why not join me?'

Her brows lifted. 'At one-thirty in the morning?'

He smiled and shrugged. 'I couldn't sleep.'

'Too much brain activity?' she suggested. 'Bill's fortunate, he can switch off at will.' She came away from the door in sudden decision. 'I will have that drink. I'm not ready for bed either. Where were you?'

'The library.' He led the way, standing back to allow her prior access to the room when they reached it. A single lamp was lit, lending soft shadows to the rest of the room. His glass stood on the side table where he had left it, an inch or more of liquid still in the bottom.

'Do you always drink doubles?' asked Claire as he poured the brandy she had requested.

'Not usually in the middle of the night,' he admitted. 'I'm not normally an insomniac either. You could be right about the brain activity. We worked through till midnight.'

'You should have objected. Or don't you have that much nerve?'

'Is nerve what it takes?' He sounded unmoved by the sarcasm. 'Attention to detail brought your father the reputation he has. Try respecting that if nothing else.'

Her head jerked up. 'He doesn't command respect.'

'He does in others.'

'You mean for his mind—his business acumen?'

'Not only that. He's a man of rare integrity.'

'Oh, honest, I'll grant you.' Her tone was bitter. 'He cares about his name all right.'

'But not about you, is that what you're saying?' Rod brought the glass across and gave it to her, looking down at her with narrowed gaze. 'You're wrong, you know. I'd say he cares a great deal. You don't make it easy for him to show it, that's all.'

'You've been in the house all of eight hours,' she responded caustically. 'What other assessments have you made?'

'None yet. I'm still working on them.' He took a seat on the chesterfield beside her and regained his own drink. 'Cheers.'

Claire found herself conscious of his nearness in a way which left her suddenly a little unsure of herself. She sought to counteract the feeling in speech. 'Are you going to be working all day tomorrow too?'

'Part of it, certainly.' The pause was brief. 'We should

be through by midday. I suppose you'll be out with the boy-friend?'

'If you mean Peter,' she said, 'he isn't *the* boy-friend.'

'I wonder how I got that impression.'

She shrugged. 'Probably from Bill. You might have gathered he disapproves.'

'Then why not tell him he doesn't have anything to worry about?'

'Why should I? My friends are my own concern.'

'He's your father.'

'But not my mentor. He opted out of that responsibility a long time ago.' Claire didn't want to talk about her father. A far more interesting subject sat right next to her. 'I don't suppose you have much time for close relationships in your line of work,' she said. 'Is that why you never married?'

'Maybe I just never met the right girl,' he returned. 'She'd have to be pretty special.'

'In looks?'

'Not essentially. I meant to take the kind of life style I could offer a woman. I don't have a settled home.'

'And you'd expect her to go with you?'

'Wherever possible, yes. Not much point in it otherwise.' There was mockery in his smile. 'Not thinking of applying, by any chance?'

She laughed. 'Just curious.'

'It's been known to kill the cat.'

'I never lost a life yet.' She put down her glass and stretched lazily, watching him out of the corner of her eye. 'You must find yours very frustrating at times, stuck miles from anywhere for weeks on end.'

'I manage.' His shoulders were relaxed against the leather, his legs comfortably stretched. Something in her knew a sudden desire to disrupt that equanimity. She put out a finger and laid it lightly over the firm mouth, her voicè very soft. 'Poor man, having to work on your last weekend. It shouldn't be allowed!'

He reached up and took hold of her hand, his grasp warm and excitingly strong as he drew her to him. The touch of his lips made her quiver. It took all her willpower to stop herself from responding more than fleetingly to the kiss before pushing him away with a jeering little laugh.

'You can think about the rest when you're up to your eyes in mud in Tanzania!'

There was little change of expression in his face, and Claire had a sudden disconcerting feeling that he had known her intention from the first. When he took her by the shoulders she thought he was about to demand a fitting retribution. Finding herself face down across his knee came as a shock which temporarily robbed her of her wits.

In all her life, Claire had never imagined anything could hurt the way that hand of his did. It took her breath, choking her cries in her throat. He kept it up for what seemed like a lifetime before finally yanking her upright again.

'There's more than one way to relieve frustration,' he said on a note of satisfaction. 'On the whole, I'd say I enjoyed that best.' Amusement quirked his lips at her expression. 'First time ever, was it? I might have guessed. Pity Bill didn't do it years ago!'

The pain was still with her, but it took second place to humiliation right then. She could hardly get the words out. 'You'll be looking for another job when he hears about this! Who do you think you are!'

'The man who just gave a self-centred little egotist the surprise of her life,' he came back sardonically. 'And don't count on the other. If you're so convinced the business comes first you can hardly expect him to fire me because I put his daughter across my knee.'

'We'll see about that!'

'No, we won't, because you won't be telling him. You'd hate to take the risk of hearing him say it to your face.'

Claire bit her lip, knowing what he said was true. Bill might not condone the action, but he was certainly not going to jeopardise an important job in order to underline the fact. 'You're so sure of yourself, aren't you?' she said bitterly.

'There's only one thing I'm sure of, you'll think twice before playing that kind of game again.' He stood up, pulling the belt of his robe tighter about his middle. 'I should sleep now all right. There's nothing like exercise for clearing the mind.'

'I hope your damned bridge falls on you!' was all Claire could find to shoot after him as he went to the door.

Rod turned his head to look back at her, his smile slow. 'I'm sure you do. Don't stay down too long, you need your beauty sleep. See you tomorrow some time.'

Not if she had anything to do with it, Claire thought in wry acknowledgment after the door had closed behind him. There was no way she was going to be able to take that mockery of his again. She would get up early in the morning and drive over to stay with Jan Chadwick for the rest of the weekend; it would be easy enough to find some reasonable excuse.

Getting to her feet, she gave a small, sharp exclamation, loathing filling her mind. If only there were some way of getting back at him! But there wasn't. He had the whip hand in every respect.

So stay and face him, the better part of her suggested. Pretend it never happened. She knew she wouldn't. She didn't have that kind of courage. Her only hope was that she never had to meet Rod Gilvray again.

CHAPTER TWO

IF life had been pointless before it seemed even more so in the weeks following. On one occasion Claire even found herself asking her father if he could find her a job of some kind at the central offices, a suggestion he viewed with an unflattering lack of enthusiasm.

'You don't know anything about what's involved,' he said. 'It would mean somebody showing you the ropes from the ground up. If you're so keen to take an interest in the business try a course at business training college, and then we'll see what can be done.'

'You don't think I'd stick it, do you?' she said shrewdly, and gained a shrug along with the wry smile.

'I'm pretty sure you wouldn't.'

Claire was pretty sure she wouldn't too. She was by no means lacking in intelligence, but repetitiveness of any kind always threw her. What she needed was a job where every day brought something totally different, and those weren't easy to come by.

In the end it was Peter who offered the most attractive proposition. 'Marry me,' he said, 'and we'll have three months' honeymoon going anywhere you like. We're two of a kind, Claire. We both think life's there for enjoying. We can have a great time for a few years before we even think about settling down.'

Bill reacted predictably when she imparted the news that same evening, but she remained adamant.

'I'm of age,' she said. 'And it's my life. You should be pleased to have me off your hands at last.'

He looked at her helplessly for a long time before replying to that one.

'Claire, I know I haven't been all a father should be,' he said at last. 'I should have spent more time with you—got to know you better. Building up the firm was as much for you as for myself. If I got my priorities wrong, I'm sorry.'

'It doesn't really matter now, does it?' she responded flatly. 'You can close down the house and move back to town once I'm gone.'

He seemed to give up then, to reconcile himself to the idea. 'When is it to be?'

'Next month. We neither of us want a big fancy wedding. You'll be back from Africa by the twelfth, won't you?'

Something flickered for a moment in his eyes. 'I'll make sure of it.'

He left a week later on the twenty-seventh. Breakfasting alone again the following morning, Claire thought dryly that at least this pattern would cease to exist for her in a fortnight's time. Marrying Peter might not be the ideal escape, but it *was* an escape. It might even turn out to be the best thing she had ever done in the long run.

The cable arrived on the morning of the 1st. Louise brought it up to Claire's room, face concerned.

'I hope it isn't bad news, miss,' she said.

The name on the bottom of the sheet was the first thing which caught Claire's eye. She felt her heart jerk. There was only one reason why Rod Gilvray would be sending her a cable. She read the brief, all too succinct message with a sense of numbness, unable at first to register any kind of emotion at all.

'My father has been injured in a rock fall,' she said. 'I have to go to him.' She threw back the bedcovers and swung her feet to the floor, sitting there for a moment barely knowing where to start. 'I'll have to find out about flights. Start packing for me, will you, Louise. My passport is in the drawer over there. Lucky I had it renewed.' She pressed a hand to her head, trying to bring some order to a confused mind. 'I'll need currency too. And I'm not sure about visas. I'd better phone Cooks.'

Events moved at a pace which left little time for rational thought after that. Claire was at the airport with only fifteen minutes before boarding her flight when she realised she had done nothing about contacting Peter. She phoned from the departure lounge, forced to content herself with leaving a message when she discovered he was out. She would cable him from Dar es Salaam as soon as she had some definite information to hand. In the meantime she had other things to think about than her forthcoming wedding.

On the plane she tried to sort out her emotions. How was she going to feel if Bill died? The answer didn't take so much searching for. She wanted him to live: very desperately she wanted him to live. They had their differences and probably always would, but he was her father. For the first time in years that really meant something. If he came through this accident she would try to reach a closer relationship with him somehow, no matter who had to make the concessions.

They landed at Dar es Salaam just after sunrise. With only one suitcase and her papers in order, Claire found herself through formalities within half an hour. Coming out to the arrivals hall, she was surprised to hear her name announced over the tannoy system, but went obediently to the information desk as instructed. A middle-aged, powerfully built man in faded denim coveralls straightened from his casual leaning position against it on her approach, glance straying over her trim figure and slim, shapely legs beneath the linen skirt with unconcealed approval. He said something to the man behind the desk before moving forward to intercept her.

'Miss Naughton?' he asked in an unmistakable Canadian accent. 'I've got the plane waiting all ready fuelled up as instructed. We can be on our way inside half an hour, unless you want breakfast first?'

Claire shook her head, more than a little bemused by the development. 'I had it on the plane. I thought my father would have been brought here to hospital by now.'

'Sorry, I don't know anything about that. My instructions were to meet you here and fly you out to Mgala pronto. Take a couple of hours or so, that's all.' He paused, studying her. 'Nothing much out there except the mine. Works for the Company, does he?'

'He was injured on the construction site,' Claire said, her heart sinking at the implications. If they still hadn't transferred Bill to the coast that must mean he was too ill to be moved—or already dead. She hastily shut off that line of thought. 'We'd better get moving, then.'

The transport was a four-seater Piper painted a shimmering white with a blue stripe. By the time they were in the air again the temperature was already rising steadily towards the lower seventies, the sun a bright ball of fire well clear of the horizon. Claire had a brief glimpse of the coastline and the city itself before they turned inland to the grass and thorn brush of the Masai Steppe.

At any other time the journey over totally new country would have interested her to the exclusion of everything else. Under the circumstances she scarcely noticed the scenery below at all, even when they left the line of the Great North Road and took to a wilderness which looked almost totally unpopulated. It was left to the pilot to tell her that the mountains vaguely discernible on the northern horizon were the Usambaras where most of Tanzania's tea came from. Worth a visit, he said, if she had the time. He seemed to be trying to take her mind off her obvious pre-occupation.

Claire still couldn't understand why there had been no more detailed message waiting for her at the airport. Surely Rod must realise how she would be feeling? On the other hand, would he? So far as he knew, her regard for her father left a whole lot to be desired. He would probably be surprised that she had even bothered to respond to his summons. All the same, surely it would have cost him nothing to let her know the true position, even if the news was of the worst. At least she would have been spared this agony of waiting.

The plateau below grew rougher, split by a ravine which wound its way tortuously in the general direction of their flight path. When the construction camp finally came in sight it was easy to pick out because it was the only sign of civilisation in the immediate area. Both end spans of the bridge were already in position, she noted, men at work on them.

The mine and its supporting township were some kilometres further west, the pilot explained, pointing out the line of the roadway curving the shoulder of a low hill before running on southwards.

'Going to make a big difference to the area this bridge across the gorge here,' he added. 'Cuts off a hundred miles or so of road when they bring in the spur from this side. Pay for itself, I'd think, if what they say about this new phosphate strike holds good. Richest in East Africa by all accounts. Some concession! Did you say your father works for the construction company?'

'Yes.' Claire saw no point in going into further detail. She could see the landing strip for which they were heading now, some half a mile distant from the site. As they passed over the latter, figures paused in their activities to look up at the plane, and one or two arms were lifted in greeting. Apparently any kind of visitor was a novelty out here.

The landing was bumpy but completed without mishap. As the Piper rolled to a stop, Claire unfastened her seat-belt and pushed open the near door, feeling the heat hit her solidly in the face. She was on the ground watching the approaching cloud of dust from the direction of the camp resolve itself into the shape of a jeep driven fast along a dirt track by the time her pilot brought round her suit-case. The latter handed over a manilla packet along with it.

'Nearly forgot about this,' he said. 'I was told to give it to you when we arrived, not before. Can't hang about, I'm afraid—got another job on this afternoon. Hope you find everything okay.'

'Thanks,' she said. 'I hope so too.'

She stood to one side as the plane taxied away to turn into the wind, her case at her feet, the envelope as yet unopened in her hand. The arrival of the jeep at her back gave her no time to start perusing the contents. Whatever was in it could wait for a more opportune moment.

The driver was a man in his mid-twenties, dressed in dusty denims and an open-necked shirt. Tousled fair hair crowned a face which at present wore an expression of un-disguised astonishment as he looked at Claire.

'Are you real?' he asked. 'Or am I having hallucinations?'

Behind her the plane began its run to take-off with a sudden increased roar of power, the note dropped as it became airborne. Claire said blankly, 'Aren't I expected?'

'Expected?' He shook his head, looking blank himself. 'Not that I'm aware of. Sure you haven't come to the wrong place?'

If she had it would have been too late now. Her transport was already heading east at a fast rate of knots. 'This is the

Naughton Construction site?' she asked, aware that it had to be.

'That's right.' He sounded as puzzled as she felt. 'Who did you want to see?'

'My father,' she said. 'I had a cable about an accident—a rock fall.'

If anything his mystification increased. 'News to me. The only accident we've had was a couple of weeks ago, and that was no rock fall. Who is your father?'

'I'm Claire Naughton,' she said.

His expression underwent an abrupt alteration. 'The boss? But he left two days ago. If he's had an accident it sure wasn't here!'

She stared at him in bewilderment. 'I don't understand. Rod Gilvray sent for me—he arranged transport here for me. What's going on?'

'I couldn't say, miss. Maybe you'd better come and ask him yourself.'

'I certainly will,' she said. Her mind was in a turmoil, unable to make any sense of what she had heard. 'I most certainly will!'

The driver got out and came round to fetch her suitcase, slinging it into the back along with the safety helmet which had been occupying the front passenger seat. With her seated beside him, he turned the vehicle to head back along the track towards the neat grouping of prefabricated buildings which constituted the camp site.

There was no conversation on the run. There seemed little to say. Her driver seemed relieved when they at last drew up in front of what appeared to be the office block.

'Gilvray's in there,' he said. 'First door. What would you like me to do with your case?'

'Hang on to it,' she said, getting out of the jeep under the fascinated gaze of those men in the vicinity. 'I'm not sure just what this is all about, but if my father isn't here I'll obviously not be staying long. First door, did you say?'

'That's right.' He stayed where he was watching her as she went into the building.

The door in question was painted green. Claire threw it open without bothering to knock, taking the two men bending over the desk inside by surprise. Rod Gilvray was the first to react, his expression a study in blank astonishment.

'What the devil are *you* doing here?' he demanded.

'I'm beginning to wonder,' she said. 'Where's my father?'

His brows drew together. 'On his way back to England, I imagine. He left a couple of days ago.'

Her breath came out on a sharp sound. 'You mean it isn't true he was injured?'

'Injured? Not that I know of.' There was sudden concern in his voice. 'What did you hear?'

'You know very well what I heard—or rather read! You sent that cable!'

'*I* sent *you* a cable?' There was no doubting the genuineness of his tone. 'Is this some kind of joke?'

'I don't know.' Claire looked at him helplessly, barely noticing the other man's presence. She felt completely at a loss. 'I had a cable in your name saying Bill had been injured in a rock fall and I was to come at once. If you didn't send it, who did?'

Rod shook his head slowly, his regard narrowed to her face. 'I can't imagine,' he said. And then on a slightly altered tone, 'Claire, if this turns out to be one of your tricks ...'

'Tricks?' She was incensed, her whole body rigid with anger and hurt. 'I just spent the most miserable few hours of my whole life getting here! Do you think I'd do that just for the pleasure of getting at you in some way? How is it supposed to work anyway?'

'I'm not sure,' he admitted. 'Right now, I'm not sure about anything. Who'd stand to benefit from a damned fool thing like this?'

'I think you ought to sit down,' put in the other man, speaking for the first time since Claire's entry into the room. His gaze was sympathetic. 'We can sort out who's responsible later after you've recovered from the shock. I'm Derek Loxley, by the way, resident engineer.'

Claire accepted his advice gratefully, conscious of her trembling limbs. She felt close to tears, relief mingling with the burning anger of realisation. Bill was all right. He wasn't dead. She had to be thankful for that at least.

'Can I have a drink?' she asked on a husky note. 'That dust out there got into my throat. Water will do.'

'We can do better than that.' He switched on an intercom set and spoke into it. 'Send some coffee over, will you, Arn? Enough for three. And make it good and strong.'

Rod was still on his feet and still wearing a look of suspicion. 'Assuming you arrived in the plane that went over a while ago, who set that up?' he asked shortly.

'I assumed you had,' she responded, borrowing his tone. She paused there in sudden recollection, reaching into her carry-all for the envelope she had deposited there. 'The pilot gave me this when he landed—said he'd been told to wait till then. I thought it rather odd.'

'But not enough to open it right away.'

'I was more interested in getting to see Bill right then.' She gave him a glance of pure dislike. 'Just get it out of your head that I'm here on any kind of pretence, will you? I've no more idea of what this is all about than you say you have.'

'If you open that envelope,' he came back equably, 'we might both find out.'

Claire clamped her lips together and did so, tearing

across the stiff sealed flap with fingers strengthened by anger. There were two smaller envelopes inside, one addressed to herself and the other to Rod Gilvray. Both were in her father's distinctive hand.

'I don't understand,' she said in bewilderment, looking from one to the other. 'This gets crazier!'

Rod reached over and took the envelope bearing his name from her, slitting a finger beneath the flap to slide out the single sheet of paper within. He had read what it had to say before Claire even had her envelope opened, his jaws tautening ominously. 'What the hell?' he exclaimed, and started to read it again, more slowly this time.

Claire dropped her eyes to the letter her envelope had contained, seeing the words leap up at her as if each one held a blow—which they did.

Dear Claire, Bill had written. *By the time you read this you'll know that the message you received was a ruse on my part. A cruel one, I know, but there was no other way I could think of to get you on that plane. Even then, I had to take a chance on you having enough feeling for me to bother, which in the face of our general relationship might be open to doubt. The truth is, I'd do anything to stop you marrying a man you don't even love, much less respect as a person. Marriage isn't something two people should enter into lightly on the premise that divorce is readily available if it doesn't work out. I never married again because I never found any woman to match your mother, and I wasn't willing to settle for less than I'd known. When you marry I want it to be to someone who will make you feel the way I did about your mother, and vice versa, and the prime requirement is to stay single until you meet him. Which is why I'm instructing Rod Gilvray to keep you there at Mgala until you come to your senses about St John. If*

*he can find you something to do around the camp all to
the good. You need something constructive to occupy
your mind. I shall be taking the liberty of cancelling the
wedding plans on the grounds that you changed your
mind—which I'm confident you will. For the rest, just
remember that I wouldn't be doing this if I didn't so
desperately want your happiness. Love, Bill.*

It was a moment or two before Claire could bring herself
to lift her eyes from the page. Rod was watching her with
a sardonic expression on his face.

'I gather the situation has been made clear to you,' he
commented. 'Bill might have left it a little late to start
putting his foot down, but when he makes a move he
certainly goes all the way!'

'Not enough for it to make any difference,' Claire retorted, pulling herself together. 'He must be mad if he
thinks I'm going to stay here a minute longer than it
takes you to get a plane out to take me back to the coast!
And you'd better start doing that right now!'

'My first reaction was similar,' Rod admitted. 'I'm not
paid to act nursemaid to anybody's offspring. On the other
hand ...' he paused, watching her expression alter with a
certain grim humour ... 'it certainly wouldn't do you any
harm to spend a few days doing something useful by way
of a change. How about it, Derek? Think we can fix her up
with a job in the camp?'

Claire briefly met the other man's eyes and shook her
head to the disconcertion in them. 'Don't worry, he's just
saying it for the sake of it. There's no way anyone can
make me stay here, and he knows it!'

'Don't take bets on it,' Rod advised with deceptive
quietness. 'And don't refer to me in the third person while
I'm around to speak for myself. I can't say I agree with
Bill's prime motive—I think you're entitled to marry who

the devil you like—but having gone to all this trouble to set it up I'd say he merits at least a token gesture. A week should be about right.'

She stared at him, unable to believe he could be even remotely serious. 'Don't talk such rot,' she said at length on a scornful note. 'Even if you had the authority you wouldn't have the nerve!'

'I do have the authority,' he reminded her, tapping the letter he still held in one hand. 'As to the other ...' He left it there, his smile faint. 'I said a week. Maybe it should be longer.'

There was warmth in her face; she could feel it under her skin. He had the nerve all right. He had proved that already. All the same, she had no intention of allowing a discomfiting memory to throw her. She glanced to Derek Loxley, for the first time taking stock of him as a person. He was older than Rod, perhaps in his early forties, and smaller in build, with thin but pleasant features beneath sandy hair. At the moment he was looking somewhat bemused, and she could scarcely blame him. She summoned her most appealing smile.

'Mr Loxley, I'm sure you must be wondering what on earth is going on.'

'I think I might have the gist of it,' he said with some reticence. 'Your father appears to have an unusual sense of humour.' His eyes moved to Rod, taking on some additional expression. 'I'm not sure what you're playing at exactly, but for God's sake let's call it a day, shall we?'

The other lifted a brow. 'Who's playing? If the boss says she's to stay, then she's staying.'

'Now who's talking in the third person?' Claire asked with irony, and received the barest of glances.

'Shut up,' said Rod. His eyes went back to the engineer, a glint of what could be amusement in them. 'I don't want to start pulling rank, but as project manager I have the say in what goes concerning the actual site operation. We're short of help in the mess, as always. I can't think of a better place to put her.'

The arrival of the coffee seemed almost on cue. It was borne by a grizzle-haired man wearing an off-white jacket and trousers whose expression was anything but affable.

'What's with the delivery service?' he demanded, setting down his burden of coffee pot and mugs on the littered desk without bothering to clear any space for them. 'You've got the makings over here when you want it.'

'But not the time to use them,' Derek turned equably. 'I asked you to send it, not bring it.'

'I would have if there'd been anybody about to send. I've got thirty-eight mouths to think about and damn-all help!'

'That's a situation about to be remedied,' Rod put in before the other man could answer. 'Meet your new kitchen hand, Arn. She's just raring to go!'

The newcomer glanced sideways in the direction indicated, seeing Claire for the first time. His expression was a study. 'Sorry, miss,' he proffered, obviously trying to recall just what he had said since he entered the room. 'Didn't notice you behind the door there.' Rod's words registered suddenly bringing a confusion which gave way swiftly to a grin. 'Some joke!'

'It's no joke. Miss Naughton is here to work.'

'Naughton?' The inflection was curious.

'That's right. Call it a family decision.' Rod seemed to be enjoying himself, one leg thrown across the corner of the desk to take his weight in an easy stance that made Claire want to kick him, his arms folded across his chest. 'Bill was here to discuss it a couple of days ago, among other things.'

'Cut it out,' Claire said brusquely, deciding it was time to put a stop to the whole charade. 'Others might not appreciate your type of humour.'

The grey regard came to rest on her. 'While you do, of course.'

'About as much as I appreciate my father's!'

'An improvement already. That's the first time I've heard you acknowledge his status in so many words.'

She was sitting on the extreme edge of her chair, nerves as taut as a drum. 'I'm telling you to stop it! It's gone far enough! I wouldn't be surprised if you and Bill concocted the whole damned thing between you while he was here. You're just about on a par when it comes to something like this. It wouldn't occur to either of you that I just spent twenty-four hours believing he might be dead.' The quiver in her voice was hastily controlled. 'You can both go to hell!'

There was a short, electric silence. Rod was the first to break it, the taunting quality gone from his voice.

'All right, you made your point. We'll talk about it later.' He took hold of the coffee pot with a forceful gesture betokening a held-in anger of his own, pouring it strong and black into one of the mugs. 'Drink this and calm down.'

Claire took it from him because she needed it, almost scalding her tongue on the too hot liquid. Catching the camp cook's eye, she forced a smile. 'It's good.'

'Thanks.' He seemed at a loss for anything else to say. 'Better be getting back,' he added after another moment's silence.

He looked glad to go. Claire wished Rod would go with him. She had a feeling the only really sympathetic ear she was going to find around here belonged to the one man who didn't work for Naughtons. Perhaps the former sensed it too, for he only took a couple of mouthfuls of his own coffee mug before setting it down with an air of getting to grips with the situation.

'I'd like to talk to Claire on her own,' he said to Derek Loxley. 'We can pick up on this again after lunch.'

Claire said tautly, 'There's nothing we have to say in private.'

'Oh, yes, there is.' His tone was unequivocal. 'This is Naughton business.'

'I hadn't noticed that particular fact bother you over-much up to now.'

'So I changed my mind.' He gave Derek a steady look. 'If you don't mind.'

There was little doubt as to whose office they were in at present, and the other man was in no position to dispute matters.

'If I weren't sure you were perfectly capable of taking care of your own interests, I'd say don't worry about a thing,' he said to Claire before he went out. 'There's no-body can keep you here against your will.'

Green eyes clashed with grey as the door closed behind him, refusing to give an inch. 'He's right, of course. If you tried it you'd be one man against many.'

'Don't count on that,' Rod came back. 'The men out there all work for your father, and they're loyal to the last man. If I tell them he wants you to stay, believe me, you'll stay.'

She didn't believe him, but it was pointless arguing a point which wasn't about to arise. She said instead, 'If you're ready to start apologising I'm ready to listen.'

His jaw hardened. 'You know, I'm only just beginning to realise what Bill's been up against with you. You don't profit from experience.'

'Meaning I'm supposed to regard you with some kind of wary reverence because of a stunt you pulled over a

month ago?' she retorted with rather more dismissive contempt than she could actually bring herself to feel over
the incident in question. 'Sorry to disappoint you, but
I'm not that easily impressed.'

His smile was a threat in itself. 'No?'

'No.' She had herself well in hand now, her lip curling
with deliberate imitation. 'Try it again and I'll put *my*
knee where it will do *you* the most good!'

It was difficult to assess his reaction. He simply stood
there gazing at her contemplatively. 'You're right,' he said
at length. 'You call for a tougher line. That spell in the
kitchen I was talking about earlier will do for starters. We
don't have electric dishwashers here. A few days up to your
elbows in hot greasy water should take some of the stuffing
out of you.'

'It might,' she admitted, 'if you could get me there.'

The shrug came easily. 'You don't work, you don't eat.
That a good enough incentive for you?'

Some new quality about him arrested her reply. She
looked at him for a long moment, taking in the hard edge
to his mouth, the cool intent in the grey eyes. 'You really
mean it, don't you?' she said with faint disconcertion.

'I do now. I don't entirely agree with the way Bill went
about things, but he would have realised that any distress he
caused you would be shortlived. Apart from that he has my
total sympathy. You're a pain in the neck, Claire. You
don't give a damn about anyone or anything.' He was speaking with a quiet control far more emphatic than any raised
voice. 'But you're going to. You don't get out of here till
you learn to appreciate what he's done for you—and why.'

She kept herself in check with an effort, feeling the
sting of the words without revealing any reaction. 'I think
Derek Loxley might have something to say about that.'

'He can say whatever he likes. He doesn't have any juris-
diction over the running of the camp, only the job itself.

His main interest is the same as mine—to bring the job in on time. He isn't going to jeopardise that for any spoiled brat, much as he might want to.' He straightened abruptly. 'If you've finished with that coffee we'd better find you somewhere to sleep. I'll move in with some of the men and you can have my bunk.'

'Such old-fashioned gallantry,' she mocked, and drew a far from old-fashioned glance sliding over her from head to foot and back again, leaving her feeling mentally if not physically stripped.

'You're safe enough on that score,' he said. 'Nice to look at maybe, but I ask for rather more than that in a girl. You might run into a little trouble with some of the men. If any of them try anything on, let me know and I'll sort it out.'

Claire stayed where she was, the bravado slowly trickling away. He wasn't kidding about any of this. He meant to make her go through with it. Backing down went against the grain, yet so did the thought of spending any more time in this place than she absolutely had to. She said resignedly, 'All right, what do I have to say to get out of here?'

'There's nothing you can say,' he returned. 'Nothing I'd believe. The day you start trying to see your father's point of view we'll talk it over.'

'How are you going to know if I'm telling the truth?'

'I'll know.'

Her coolness vanished in a sudden wave of white-hot anger. The coffee mug in her hand was almost empty, but it wouldn't have mattered one iota had it been full to the brim of scalding liquid right then. Her aim was deadly—or would have been had Rod not moved his head to one side with an even swifter reaction. Coffee dregs splattered his shirt as the mug shattered on the wall behind him. He looked down at them in disgust.

'You really do Bill proud, don't you,' he said.

'Rod, I'm sorry.' The realisation of what might have happened had he not moved in time made her voice tremble. 'I've never done anything like that before in my life!'

'I'll bet.' His glance made her writhe. 'Just let it be the last, because I'll wring your neck if it happens again! Where's your luggage?'

'Outside in the jeep.' She was subdued, too disgusted with her own behaviour to protest any further over his at the moment. 'I told the driver to wait.'

The jeep was still there when they got outside, but the driver was gone. Her suitcase was in the rear seat where he had left it, the leather hot to the touch.

Rod hoisted it out and indicated another of the temporary buildings some distance away. 'Over there.'

Walking at his side through the dust of the cleared site, Claire was very much aware of the attention they were attracting. Word had probably gone round by now; it never took long. She was thankful there had been no one else present to witness her loss of control a moment or two ago. Bad enough that Rod had seen it. She felt bitterly ashamed.

The actual construction site was far enough away to keep noise to a minimum. Any time now the siren would sound to bring the men in for the midday meal. From past experience, Claire knew her father always worked to the single shift principle, avoiding the extra cost of penalty rates and additional camp accommodation in the belief that men worked better and kept fresher on regular hours. She had visited a working site before this, but some time ago and in England. Certainly the situation had been nowhere near the same. She still wasn't wholly certain how she was going to handle this one.

The room Rod had spoken of turned out to be slightly larger than a rabbit hutch, with a collapsible bed, a canvas wardrobe pack and other bare essentials. The heat was sticky, the small window aperture admitting little of the midday breeze.

'You'll have to time your visits to the showers and latrines when the men aren't around,' he said, slinging her suitcase on to the bed and beginning to collect his own things together. 'The camp generator is run three times during the day for hot water and cooking, and from dark to midnight for lighting. You'll need to develop night sight for any moving around after lights out.'

'This is getting to sound quite ridiculous.' There was a faint note of desperation in her tone. 'You can't be serious!'

'I can, and I am.' He turned to look at her, his arms full of clothing and other items, his mouth unrelenting. 'You can eat second lunch with me before you start work.'

Her own lips tightened. 'I am not working in any kitchen,' she said between her teeth, forgetting any resolutions. 'You're not going to make a fool of me!'

'So go hungry. I'll make sure Arnie understands you're not to eat until you're ready to pay for it.'

'Do you think he's going to take any notice now that he knows who I am?'

'He'd better. I can always show him Bill's letter.'

'Bill said nothing about starving me!'

'How do you know? You didn't see it. He'd hardly expect you to knuckle under without some kind of duress.' He was moving towards the door as he spoke. 'I'll come back for the rest. You've got till then to change your mind. Think about it.'

Claire sat down heavily on the bed as he went out, the events of the last twenty-four hours beginning to catch up on her. By now, in all probability, Bill would be home again. There was no doubt in her mind that he would do exactly as he had said he would. Having gone this far he was hardly going to start backing down now. She wondered how Peter would take the news, but could conjure no particular distress for him. There was even a trace of relief in the thought. She hadn't really wanted to marry him all that desperately. She had said yes to him only because there had seemed nothing better to do at the time.

But that still didn't give Bill the right to take the law in his own hands this way. Whatever his motives, he had given her a nasty shock, and she wasn't about to forgive him very easily for it. Least of all was she going to accept the set-up he'd laid out for her here, regardless of what Rod Gilvray might think. If he wouldn't make the arrangements to get her back to the coast then she would appeal to someone who would. Derek Loxley didn't seem a man to be easily intimidated. He would help her, she was sure of it.

She was still sitting in the same position when Rod came back. He eyed her questioningly.

'Well?'

'I'm not hungry,' she said.

His shrug was indifferent. 'Suit yourself. You will be. Incidentally, if you're thinking of trying to raise sympathy from any of the men, I've ordered the word passed around that you're here on your father's orders and nobody interferes if they want to keep their job. There'll be some speculation over the whys and wherefores. What you tell anyone who gets round to asking is your own concern.'

Claire let him reach the door again before saying his name very quietly, bringing his head round to look at her. 'I'll get even with you for this,' she threatened, still in the same low tone, 'if it's the last thing I ever do!'

He didn't even bother answering.

CHAPTER THREE

THE heat grew in the little room as the afternoon progressed, but Claire found herself too weary to care. She fell asleep fully clothed apart from her linen jacket, head cradled on one hand so that her dark hair fell forward almost covering her face, stockinged feet tucked under the folded edge of the light blanket at the foot of the bed.

It was dark when she awoke, and the blanket had been drawn up over her waist. She sat up stiffly, memory flooding back with an accompanying sense of rationalisation. Seen in retrospect, the whole situation became ludicrous. Now that tempers had cooled they could perhaps get down to sorting it out. Rod must have been in and covered her with the blanket at some time, which certainly seemed to suggest a change of heart. She would make sure not to antagonise him again.

In the meantime she badly needed a shower and a change of clothing. She felt disgustingly sticky and dishevelled. She tried to sort out the camp geography in her mind's eye. The water tanks had been to the rear of the building she was in at the moment, which meant that the washing facilities couldn't be far away. There were lights strung across the compound outside, and she could hear the sound of voices from no great distance. The luminous figures of her watch face told her it was five minutes past seven. She had no idea what time supper was served, but no doubt it wouldn't be late.

The thought of food brought hunger pangs to her stomach. It had been more than twelve hours since she had

41

last eaten, and with only that one mug of coffee by way of liquid refreshment. Recollection of what she had done with that mug made her flush in the darkness. She really had outclassed herself that time! A heavy object striking at such a close distance would have caused a great deal more than a headache. She could even have found herself on the wrong end of a grievous bodily harm charge, locked in a prison cell in some primitive African township.

The knock on the door seemed almost to echo her meandering thoughts. She called 'Come in' without getting to her feet, unsurprised when Rod Gilvray opened it.

'You don't have to sit in the dark,' he said, and switched on a low powered light, viewing her with an enigmatic expression without moving away from the doorway. He had changed his coffee-splattered shirt for a fresh one in a fine check open at the throat. The skin beneath was tanned and taut, with a triangle of hair showing at the apex of the V. He had his hands in the pockets of his light cotton slacks.

'Feeling rested?' he asked.

Claire nodded. 'Quite a lot. I always forget how much a jet flight can take out of one.' She paused, not at all certain what to say next. 'Did you cover me up?' was all she could think of.

'Yes,' he said. 'It gets pretty cool by comparison at night. The last thing you need is a chill.'

She smiled a little ruefully. 'The first thing I need is a good hot shower. Can it be arranged?'

'Shortly. They'll be free during supper.'

'Good. I can't say I need to work up an appetite, because I'm ravenous.' Her tone was meant to convey wry acknowledgment of their previous contretemps. 'I suppose there'll be plenty left by the time I get through?'

'Plenty,' he agreed. He sounded more relaxed. 'The mess is right next to the shower hut. If you come on through when you're ready I'll have a plate waiting. You're going to cause something of a stir with that lot out there, you realise. They've been here almost a month already, and the laid-on entertainment soon starts to pall. A woman on camp is a novelty, even if she is the boss's daughter. One or two might forget themselves.'

'I'll make sure not to encourage familiarity,' said Claire. 'Anyway it's only for one evening. I assume you can radio through for transport.'

The strong mouth straightened again. 'I could,' he said after a moment, 'if necessary. Agreeing to work is only half of it. You still have to get round to the rest.'

She stared at him in steadily growing anger, aware that nothing had changed at all during the intervening hours. 'I haven't agreed to work,' she clipped. 'And I shan't agree to it! The sooner you reconcile yourself to that the sooner we can finish this whole stupid affair! I'm going to have that shower and then I'm coming to the mess for a meal. Try to stop me and I'll show you up for the meddling fool you are!'

He didn't stir a muscle, nor did his expression alter any that she could see. 'If there's any showing to be done it will be by me,' he said. 'I mean it, Claire. I shan't give a damn who you are or where we are. If you want to risk it, go right ahead.'

She believed him. She daren't not believe him. He had her in a cleft stick and he knew it. Hunger almost made her throw in the towel there and then, but pride spoke first.

'All right, so we'll see who can hold out the longest. You might fancy yourself in the role Bill's given you right now, but there's a limit to how long even you can stand by and see somebody starve.'

His grin was sudden and unexpected. 'You know, I could admire that stubborn streak if you used it the right way.

There's no limit on liquids—that would be criminal—just
on food. People have been known to last as long as four
months without eating. I give you a maximum of two days.'

He had vanished again before she could reply. Not that
there was anything useful she could have said. If he was
being unbearable, she herself had little to be proud of, yet
it seemed to make no difference. She couldn't, she just
couldn't start giving in to him now. There had to be
another way round the deadlock.

Derek Loxley, of course. She had almost forgotten him.
As resident engineer he would have a permanent home on
camp regardless of the proximity of the owners themselves
in the shape of the mining company. And there was a
further source, should it become necessary. They would
have transport facilities. She didn't mind paying somebody to get her out of this place. In fact, she would pay
them well. She felt suddenly better about everything. Hunger would be no problem once she had contacted Derek
Loxley. He would see her right.

The sound of voices and hearty male laughter came
from the direction of the mess hut when she made her
way over to the showers some minutes later. The night air
felt pleasant on her skin, the breeze bringing unfamiliar
scents to her nostrils. They had seen little game from
the air this morning. She supposed most of it would be
concentrated around the area of the National parks. The
nearest one to here would be Ruaha, she believed. A
friend had done a safari trip to East Africa some months
ago and been full of it ever since. At any other time Claire
might have felt an interest in seeing more of the country
herself. Under the circumstances, however, all she wanted
to do was see the last of it.

She found the shower facilities utilitarian but adequate.
It was sheer luxury just to stand under warm water and

soap away the feel of twenty-four hours without a proper wash. The mirror hung above the washbasin immediately opposite her stall reflected a well-defined bone structure beneath the confining cap, reaching down as far as a pair of slim but determined shoulders and the rounded curve of her breasts. Nice to look at, Rod had said earlier. She knew that already, but it was good to have it confirmed—even by such as him. Oddly, considering their present relationship, she found herself speculating on what it might be like to have him finish the kiss he had begun some weeks ago. He would know a lot about it, there was no doubt about that. And not only kissing. Just because a man hadn't married it didn't mean he had no interest in the allied intimacies. The women who'd been through his bed were probably legend by now.

Dried again, she dressed swiftly in white cotton slacks and shirt, then ran a comb through her hair and applied a pale dash of lipstick. That would do for now. She wasn't out to impress Derek Loxley with anything but her helplessness. Carrying her soiled clothing and damp towel, she went out again into the night.

Some of the men were already leaving the mess hut. Claire approached a couple of them, with an air of confidence, ignoring the way they were looking at her.

'I want to see Mr Loxley,' she said. 'Can you tell me where I might find him?'

It was the younger of the two who answered. Only then did Claire recognise him as the one who had driven her from the plane that morning.

'The engineer's office is right next to the manager's,' he said. 'He's more often than not in there.'

'Even at this hour?'

'Sure.' The grin was infectious. 'Likes his own company most of the time. Daresay he'll not object to yours, though. Not many would.'

Claire smiled back. 'There are always exceptions. Thanks, anyway. I'll go and see.'

'Come back if he isn't there,' he called after her, 'and I'll help you look for him.'

He was there, however. At least, there was a light in the window. Claire made her way past the first door on the left to the second, knocking tentatively before putting her head round it.

'Mind if I come in?' she asked.

The engineer came swiftly to his feet as she followed her words with the action without bothering to wait for confirmation. 'I wondered where you'd got to,' he said. 'You haven't been to the mess yet?'

'I haven't been allowed.' She barely needed to emphasise the plaintiveness. She paused. 'How well do you know my father, Mr Loxley?'

'We met for the first time this week when he came to take a look at the job,' he said. 'And the name is Derek.'

'I know.' Her smile was warm. 'I just wasn't certain how much of a friend you were likely to be, put to the test.'

'Try me,' he invited. 'I'm not all that sure what's going on between you and Gilvray, but if I can be of any help at all ...'

'Oh, you can. You really can!' Claire sat down suddenly on the nearby chair as if her legs would no longer support her. 'I'm sorry, I think I must still be suffering from shock. Or perhaps it's hunger.'

'You haven't eaten at all?' It was he who sounded shocked now.

She shook her head. 'Not a bite in more than fourteen fours. Rod Gilvray and my father have one thing in common—they neither of them know where to draw the line. You see, it all began with Bill—my father—taking a dislike to the man I'm going to marry. You probably gathered the rest.'

'More or less. Not that it makes it any easier to understand. I've a daughter of my own. There's no way I could ever put her through what you must have gone through no matter how much I disapproved of her choice of a husband.'

A pang shot through her. 'Are you very close?'

'I think so. We spend a lot of time together when I'm home.'

'That must be nice for you both.' There was a genuine wistfulness in her voice. 'Bill and I never were, not in any way that counted. Perhaps I'm as much to blame. I should have tried harder.'

'Tell me about it,' invited Derek, sitting down again himself. He opened a drawer and took out a bar of chocolate, pushing it across to her. 'That's the best I can do at the moment. Once the men have cleared the mess we'll go over and sort things out with friend Gilvray.'

The chocolate tasted wonderful, the coffee he poured for her from the thermos pot at his elbow even better. He always brought some over with him when he came to work, he told her. This was the one time of day when he could be sure of freedom from interruption. Before she knew it, Claire found herself telling him the story of her life, letting out the bitterness and resentment in a way she had never done before with anyone.

'I should have studied civil engineering myself,' she finished on a wry note. 'It's open to women these days. At least that way we might have achieved some kind of balance.'

'You might.' Derek sounded doubtful about it. 'That kind of relationship usually only works with a son. A daughter should mean something entirely different to a father. I know mine does.'

'Then I envy her,' she said. There was a small silence. When she spoke again it was on a forcibly lighter note. 'At least I feel I have an ally in camp now. You're a nice man, Derek.'

He went a little pink, his eyes not quite meeting hers. 'I'm a disgusted one, at the moment,' he said. 'I can't say I get along with Gilvray all that well at the best of times, but this beats all. The man must be mad if he thinks he can really get away with it!'

'Not mad,' she returned. 'Just despotic.'

'Well, not any more. I'll see to that. First we get you something to eat, then we see about arranging transport out for tomorrow. It's going to add to overheads, but that's your father's look-out, I'm afraid.' He stood up, not all that much taller than her own five feet five. 'Shall we go?'

The mess hall was much as Claire had imagined it, with rows of easily-cleaned metal tables and chairs and a few posters scattered about the walls to brighten it up. The kitchen premises lay to the rear behind a serving zone. Arnie and a slightly younger man were already at work clearing up the debris from the evening meal. The former watched them coming with resignation plainly written on his features.

'Miss Naughton didn't get any supper, Arnie,' said Derek. 'What can you do for her?'

'Supper's over,' came the answer on a defensive note.

'I know that, man. I'm asking you to rustle something up. Something quick like ham and eggs, perhaps?' The last with an enquiring glance in Claire's direction.

'Lovely,' she agreed. She was watching Arnie, trying to make him look directly at her. 'Ham and eggs will do just fine.'

'The boss said nothing,' he came back, still avoiding her eyes. 'Can't do anything without his say-so.'

'You mean the camp foreman?' asked Derek, and received an aggrieved glance from the cook.

'You know who I mean as well as I do.'

'If you really want to start splitting hairs,' Claire put in, losing patience, 'there's only one real boss, and that's my father.'

This time Arnie did look at her, an air of apology about his expression. 'He's not here, miss. Gilvray is. What he says goes. That's the way it works.'

'Not for me it doesn't.' Derek had also lost patience. He started forward. 'I'll cook the damned stuff myself if needs be! Have a seat, Claire, it won't take long. I'm pretty good with a frying pan.'

The other man had vanished, leaving the stack of greasy pans to their fate. Arnie stood irresolute for a moment or two while the engineer opened doors and found the ingredients he was looking for, then he shrugged and turned away with a look which said, Let them get on with it.

Perched on a corner of the preparation table, Claire watched her rescuer lay succulent slices of ham in the huge frying pan and put it over the flame. There were two cookers run off Calor gas, plus a couple of refrigerators. No roughing it with food cooked over wood stoves for the Naughton teams. They had the best field facilities available—another of her father's policies which had paid off. A job with Naughtons was considered the cream on the doughnut. Small wonder if Arnie had no desire to risk his.

'I should really be doing that, I suppose,' she said. 'It's what most men would call a woman's work.'

Derek laughed. 'I'm not most men. I always cook breakfast at home. My wife cremates bacon if she's left to it— comes from trying to read the morning paper at the same time. One job at a time, that's my motto.'

They were still laughing when Rod walked in via the rear door. Meeting the grey eyes, Claire felt her whole face stiffen.

'Out,' he said succinctly.

Derek answered for her, his face set into lines which

boded ill for the next few minutes. 'She stays right here. Lay a finger on her, and you'll have me to reckon with!'

Considering his lack of inches compared with the other man, the statement was doubly admirable, Claire reflected. She slipped from the table to stand on her feet, determination in her lifted chin.

'Why don't you just forget the whole idea?' she suggested. 'Your job is safe enough. Bill's wanted you on his payroll for too long to let this get in the way.'

'I'm not doing it for Bill,' he came back grimly. 'Not any longer. This is just between the two of us.'

'Not while I'm around it isn't.' Derek had turned round from the cooker, leaving the ham to look after itself, the metal slice looking faintly ridiculous held as a weapon. 'For God's sake, man, leave it alone, will you? You've already gone too far.'

He was ignored. Rod held the door open, his attention wholly for Claire. 'I said outside.'

She saw Derek's movement out of the corner of her eye and gave a sharp exclamation. 'Don't!' The regard she levelled at Rod held contempt. 'He's a judo black belt. I'm sure he wouldn't hesitate to use it.'

'I've done a bit of that myself,' claimed the other man, but there was an element of doubt in his voice. 'I'm not letting you get away with this, Gilvray!'

'It's all right, Derek.' Claire used the name deliberately. 'I'm not having any trouble caused over me.' She smiled at him with genuine gratitude. 'Thanks anyway. We both know who's the better man.'

Rod was listening to the exchange with a sardonic twist to his lips. 'Cut and print,' he said. 'You couldn't improve on that performance.' His eyes went beyond her as she moved towards him, coming to rest on the sizzling pan. 'Supplies aren't due in for another three days. If we run short on ham we'll know who to blame.'

'Stop nit-picking,' Claire responded witheringly, reaching him. 'My father doesn't run that tight an operation.'

'He isn't running this,' came the equally withering answer. 'I am. Food wastage adds hundreds to overheads on every job.'

The smell of the cooking ham tantalised her nostrils, contracting her stomach muscles. It took every ounce of willpower she possessed to stop herself from begging him to let her stay and eat it. The only way she was going to get her teeth into that meat was by accepting his ultimatum, and she wasn't quite that desperate yet.

She was overlooking the obvious, she realised almost in the same breath. Why not eat first and then refuse to pay the price? It would only work once, but now was her prime concern. She lifted a pair of resigned green eyes.

'All right, you win. I'm too hungry to care any more.'

There was no light of triumph in his gaze, just an increase in mockery. 'Arnie will keep it hot for you until you've finished.'

For Claire that was the straw which broke the camel's back. She swung at him wildly, felt her wrist caught and held and was next moment through the door and being propelled firmly across the dry grass in a grip that hurt. Rod didn't speak until they reached the room he had allocated her, pushing her inside and standing with his back against the door and a look on his face which dared her to challenge him one more time.

'Try that again,' he gritted, 'and I'll swing right back. Did you really think I'd be fool enough to fall for a trick like that?'

'You're no fool,' she said bitterly, nursing a bruised wrist. 'A sadistic bully would be closer to the mark! You're enjoying this, aren't you?'

'To a certain degree,' he admitted without turning a hair. 'You've had it coming for a long time.'

'How would you know? You barely know me!'

'I know what I've heard—what Bill's told me about you —what he said in that letter this morning.'

This morning. Was it really only bare hours ago since her arrival here? It seemed like days!

'Whatever he said,' she burst out with heat, 'it can't possibly excuse what you're doing! He'll go spare when he finds out just how far you've gone!'

Rod took the folded sheet of paper out of his shirt pocket and tossed it to her. 'So read it for yourself and then tell me I've misinterpreted.'

She smoothed out the letter with unsteady fingers. It wasn't long, but it was right to the point:

> *You're not going to like this, and I don't blame you, I don't have any other alternative. The truth is, I'd try anything to stop Claire marrying that no-good St John. I want you to keep her there for as long as it takes to make her see reason. How you do it is entirely up to you. Find her a job, let her get her hands dirty. It can't do any harm and it might just do her good. She's my kid, and I love her, but I sure as hell haven't been much of a father to her. Small wonder I can't handle her now.*

'Keep it,' Rod invited when she failed to look up. 'You might learn something from it if you look hard enough. There's a flask of coffee on the table there. I'll see you in the morning.'

'It isn't going to alter anything,' she said low-toned. 'I'm not going to have everyone laughing at me.'

'Because you found yourself capable of turning a helping hand? Why should anybody find that funny? They'd probably admire you for it.' He paused, eyeing her averted face, then shrugged. 'Think about it. You've got all night.'

'Going to lock the door?' she demanded with sarcasm.

'There aren't any locks. And where would you go?

That's Africa out there, not England. There's nothing between here and the coast but the odd village.'

'Tell me some news!'

'I'd tell you a whole lot of things,' he came back hardily, 'if I thought they'd get through. You're not going to win, Claire. That's one thing you can be sure of.'

She stood gazing fixedly at the closed door for a long time after he had gone, the letter still gripped in her hand. Betrayal was a dramatic word, but that was how she felt. He loved her, Bill said. How could he if he would do this to her?

And Rod? It was true what she'd said; he was enjoying the whole affair. Even more would he enjoy her humiliation. But she would show him. She would show them both. Nothing between here and the coast maybe, but there was the mine and township to the west. If she could get her hands on one of the camp jeeps she could be there in no time. Someone would help her. For enough money one could always find a willing hand.

She waited until after the generator shut down at midnight before making a move, taking the bare minimum with her in the carry-all she had brought from the plane. Without lighting it was difficult to get her bearings, the lack of a moon both help and hindrance. After a moment or two she stopped to give her eyes time to adjust, leaning against the side of the nearest hut with the bag at her feet.

The silence of the plains could almost be felt, broken only by the occasional far-off cry of some animal. The latter gave rise to some faint doubt hastily shrugged off. She would be safe enough from anything likely to be found in this area so long as she stuck to the track. Out to the airstrip and keep heading west, that was the only direction she needed. Once she struck the road she had seen from the air she was home and dry.

The flare of a match from a distance of a few feet away robbed her of what night sight she had managed to acquire. Her heart thudded painfully, steadying again as a figure too stocky to be Rod's moved away from the darker bulk of the hut.

'Leaving us so soon?' asked a voice she recognised from earlier in the evening on a bantering note. 'What did we do?'

'Not a thing.' Claire relaxed the tension in her limbs and stayed right where she was, slowly deciphering his features behind the red glow of the cigarette. If she handled this right he could be of help to her. 'I'm looking for the car pool,' she said, taking the bull by the horns. She kept her voice low but light, a smile on her lips. 'I want to go to the mine.'

'Nobody on at this time of night,' he said. 'Day shift only. Anybody special you wanted to see?'

She might as well go the whole hog having started, Claire decided. This might even turn out to be a lucky break.

'Anyone with the authority and ability to fix me up with transport to Dar es Salaam,' she declared boldly.

'Tonight? That's a tall order!'

'Even for the boss's daughter?'

His grin was just discernible. 'Well now, that might just make a difference. I know one of the Company men who might do it—for a consideration.'

'I'll pay whatever he asks,' she said.

'Better not tell him that or he'll have the lot.' He paused, the cigarette held between finger and thumb. 'Gilvray said you weren't to leave camp.'

Claire wished she could see his face more clearly. 'And what do you think about that?'

'Me?' He shrugged. 'I guess I'm all for personal choice —specially when it comes to helping out the boss's daughter. You want out, you got it.'

'You mean you'll take me to this man you spoke about?'

'I'll have to. You might find the town, you'd never find the right guy.' The cigarette went down on the ground, extinguished by the toe of a boot. 'I'll get some keys. You wait here.'

He seemed to be gone a long time, although it could only have been a few minutes. Claire let out a breath of relief when she saw he was alone.

'I thought you might have decided to report in,' she confessed, and sensed his mock indignation.

'Hey, don't you trust me?'

She had to; there was no one else. She moved with him warily, not at all loath to let him take the bag from her as they picked their way across the compound. At one point she stumbled, and felt his arm come round her waist to hoist her upright. He left it there. In the circumstances she could hardly find room to protest.

One of the jeeps was parked over near the office. He slung the bag in the back with one hand, turning her round in front of him with the other and holding her there, teeth glinting in the darkness.

'How about a consideration for me?' he suggested. 'I don't ask much. Just a kiss will do.'

For a start? Claire wondered, and made herself dismiss the thought. He wasn't the type. All he wanted was a token gesture. If it would get her away from here he could have it.

She found the touch of his lips not unpleasant, though she kept hers firmly closed. Only when his hands tightened against her back to draw her closer to him did she start to resist, bringing up her knee with just enough force to make him drop her with a sharp exclamation.

'You damned little hellcat!'

'You're so right,' agreed another voice dryly, bringing both heads swinging round. 'Hell, it is!'

Rod was so close he must have followed them across the compound, Claire realised. She felt sick with disillusionment. All for nothing. She wouldn't be going anywhere now.

Her companion was having obvious regrets of his own, seeing his job already gone. 'I'll get my gear together,' he said with resignation.

'Forget it,' he was advised in the same dry tone. 'This time. I know what you were up against. Just get out of here.'

The other man got, with alacrity. Claire leaned against the jeep bonnet with a coolness she was a long way from feeling, looking up at the hard features. 'I nearly made it,' she said.

'You were certainly trying.' The inflection seared. 'Do you draw the line at anything?'

She shrugged, refusing to let the scorn get to her. 'What's in a kiss?'

Even in the darkness she could see his expression alter— or did she merely sense it? It was a moment before he answered. When he did it was with grim intent. 'I'll show you what can be.'

So far as kissing went Claire had done her share, and enjoyed a fair percentage of it. What she had never experienced before was a kiss given in anger, and that wasn't meant to be enjoyed. She felt violated by it, shaken to the core by the sheer degradation of being forced to suffer it. The roughness of the hand covering her breast was a violation of a different kind, her senses springing alive despite herself. When she tried to bring up her knee as she had done before she found it trapped between his in a vice-like grip which rendered her totally helpless.

'Convinced?' he asked, lifting his head but leaving his hand where it was.

'Get your hands *off* me!' she muttered between her teeth.

'Why?' he demanded. 'Don't you like it? You might have got a great deal more if Braden had taken you wherever you were going.' He moved the ball of this thumb in a slow caress which set every nerve tingling. 'Maybe you wanted that to happen. Some can't help themselves.'

'Don't!' She was asking now, not telling, fighting the response he was rousing in her with a sense of disgust at her own weakness. She hated him, yet the mere touch of his hands could do this to her. 'I'm not like that.'

His release of her was sudden, as if he himself had been in the grip of that same compulsion. 'I'd like to believe you.'

'It's true. I don't sleep around.' She drew in a shuddering breath, aware of the need to convince him. 'Whatever else I might be, it isn't that!'

'Then don't try acting it,' he said harshly after a moment. 'You owe yourself that much of a regard.' He reached into the car for her bag. 'Come on. I need sleep if you don't.'

They made it back to the hut in silence. Rod didn't come into the room this time, simply saw her to the door.

'I'm on the other side of this partition,' he said, touching it with his fingertips. 'I'll hear you if you try taking off again.'

'I shan't.' Her tone was subdued. 'Just leave me alone.'

'I'd be glad to. You know how to make me.'

She looked at him then, a brief, searing glance. 'Don't you ever give up?'

'Not once I've started something, no.'

The sigh came deep. 'What time do I start?'

'Breakfast is at five. I'll give you a call at four-thirty.'

'But it's almost one now!'

'Tough.' His tone lacked sympathy. 'You'll adjust.'

Claire didn't bother to say goodnight; she couldn't have trusted herself to speak. The narrow bed looked anything but inviting, yet she couldn't deny her weariness. It hardly seemed worthwhile taking off her clothes under the circumstances. She had to force herself to make the effort.

Lying there in the darkness she thought about the man next door, trying to analyse her emotions. Dislike, resentment, antagonism—they were all there, but along with them something else; something she hated to face. After all Rod had said and done to her could she really be attracted to him?

She had to admit she could. And was. It just went to show how totally unreliable emotions could be.

CHAPTER FOUR

THE following few days were about the hardest, most wearing and yet oddly most satisfying Claire had ever spent. Catering in bulk was not in itself so difficult, she found; it was the preparation and clearing away which took all the time. The first two evenings all she wanted to do was crawl into bed after supper.

As the first novelty of her presence began to wear off a little she found herself better able to cope with the badinage from the men, developing a standard of repartee which kept them laughing and coming back for more. One of them jokingly addressed her as 'your ladyship' when thanking her for an extra large helping of apple pie, and the name stuck. Whatever the speculation regarding the reason for her being here at all, Claire knew she had been accepted, and the knowledge felt good.

Of Rod she saw little because she deliberately avoided him. Most of her off-duty time she spent talking to Derek Loxley or reading the periodicals and paperbacks scattered about the recreation room. There was a film shown most nights, and various kinds of other activities for those who wanted them. Not judo on this particular job, Claire noted. That would no doubt be reserved for the longer-term projects. This one would be completed inside another few weeks.

Sunday was a general day of rest, with mealtimes staggered accordingly. In the afternoon Derek drove Claire over to the town some five miles distant to meet the wife and young family of the mining company's general manager. She found the town itself larger than she had anticipated, with several thriving stores and a colourful bazaar. The manager and other mine executive staff had a small estate of their own on the outskirts, although only two of the men had their families with them. They appeared to enjoy a good standard of living.

'Apart from the temperature and those zebra we saw earlier, I find it difficult to believe I really am in Africa,' Claire confessed during the drive back to camp. 'I didn't expect jungle exactly, but I did imagine a more varied kind of landscape.'

'This is scrub country,' Derek explained. 'You need to go up to Kilimanjaro or down to the Selous for the real contrasts. There's plenty of animal life round here too, come to that, but not too much of the spectacular kind. Somebody said they saw a couple of rhino last weekend. I don't know whether they got a shot.'

'Shot?' she queried.

'Photograph.' His smile was without mockery. 'We didn't bring hunting licences in with us.'

'I'm glad to hear it.' She stirred in her seat, watching the sun drop with almost visible speed towards the horizon. 'It's going to be dark before we make camp.'

'We can't miss it,' he responded reasonably. 'And the track surface is good.' He glanced at her briefly. 'You trust me, don't you?'

Claire laughed. 'Of course. That thought hadn't occurred to me.'

'Because I'm old enough to be your father?'

Something in his tone pulled her up. 'Not really. My father is a good bit older than I imagine you to be. I meant you're the kind of man I feel able to trust.'

It was difficult to assess his reaction to that statement. His next question was some time in coming. 'Do you feel able to trust Gilvray the same way?'

Claire looked at him sharply. 'Why?'

'I noticed you'd been avoiding him, and I wondered, that's all.'

'It's hardly surprising, is it, considering? Not that he's getting quite the results he hoped for. I'm quite enjoying myself.'

'You are?' He sounded doubtful.

'That's right. You see, it's one in the eye for both him and my father. They probably thought a couple of days and I'd be begging to go home. Well, I'm not. I'm going to stay right on until Bill has to get in touch just to see what's happening.'

'What about your fiancé?'

Until that moment Claire had forgotten about Peter. She hadn't thought of him in days. She shrugged. 'He'll survive.'

'That doesn't sound very lover-like.'

'I know.' She had the grace to feel ashamed. 'I think marrying him would have been more of a gesture than anything. I like him, and I don't think he's quite the lightweight my father makes out, but that's no basis for marriage.' She added with a sigh, 'You're very easy to talk to, Derek.'

'Practice for when my daughter starts bringing me her problems.' His tone was light. 'At least, I hope she will.'

'How old is she?' Claire asked.

'Thirteen. Not an early maturer, thank God. She still thinks like a thirteen-year-old should.'

'No boy-friends, you mean?'

'Well, there's the boy next door. He's a year older, but they've played together since they were toddlers. I suppose I might have to start keeping an eye on him. They get too much sex education at school these days, it makes them want to experiment. In my day we knew nothing outside basic biology, and you somehow didn't start applying that to humans until much later. What sort of world is it that has to set up special clinics for eleven-year-olds!' He broke off there, smiling a little ruefully. 'Sorry about that—I tend to get a bit carried away. It's just that any parents with a young daughter have a lot more to worry about these days. You just have to hope you've managed to instil moral values.'

They talked along more general terms after that. Claire had the feeling he was a little embarrassed over his outburst, but she didn't see why. A lot of what he had said was true. She wondered if her own father had ever worried that way over her, and came to the conclusion that he couldn't have done so, as he had never once mentioned the subject. So far as he knew, she could have been having intimate relations with men for years. Rod had obviously believed her capable the other night. The antagonism stirred afresh. If only there were some way of bringing that man to his knees!

Darkness fell while they were still some two miles or so from camp. Even after several days, Claire found the swiftness of the transition remarkable. She missed the twilight period when the stars began to show one by one and the world slowly settled down. Here, it was almost like switching off a light.

The night sounds rose thick and fast about them: a constant hum which went beyond the realms of consciousness at times. With the headlights on and the canvas cover overhead, they seemed cocooned in their own private little bubble. She was almost sorry when the lights from the camp came into view.

There was a special film showing that evening, the epic *Ben Hur*, which even those who had already seen it wanted to see again. Claire sat with Derek, and Fred Gillott, the camp medic, and booed along with the rest when the projector broke down for the second time. There was no sign of Rod. No doubt he thought this kind of entertainment beneath him.

She discovered his whereabouts later when she returned to her room. He looked at her levelly from the bed where he reclined full length, hands clasped behind his head.

'Better shut the door,' he advised. 'I want to talk to you.'

Claire did so only because others were out there, leaning her back against it with a calmness she was a long way from feeling.

'You said the other night that I owed myself a good name,' she said. 'If anyone saw you coming in here how long do you think it would last?'

'Nobody saw me. You were all in the rec.' He swung his feet to the ground, coming to a sitting position. His tone was hard. 'You're spending too much time with Derek Loxley. It's drawing comment.'

'Tough.' She used the word with purpose. 'I can take it.'

'But can he?'

She stiffened. 'I don't know what you mean.'

'You know all right, you're not that dumb. I doubt if there's one man on this camp could keep his mind on a strictly platonic level given the same incentive you're giving Loxley.'

Claire lifted her brows provokingly. 'Not even one?'

He studied her for a moment before answering, mouth taking on a slant. 'I've been as long without a woman as the rest of them, and you're not built to be ignored. I'd get as much pleasure out of making love to you as Loxley would.'

She refused to let any reaction show. 'Purely on the physical side, of course.'

'Naturally. We're not exactly compatible in other departments.'

'Not in that one either!' she flashed, unable to restrain

herself, and saw his smile widen a fraction.

'If you're so convinced of that come on over here and prove it.'

Claire stared at him, feeling the rapid beat of her heart. She actually wanted to accept that invitation, she realised with a sense of shock. She wanted to feel his arms about her again, his mouth on hers. Physical, as he had said: it had to be. But no less a temptation because of it.

'Scared?' he taunted. 'Or just lacking in faith?'

It came to her then that in this way at least she could have him just where she wanted him. It would be a bit like hunting for big game—infinitely dangerous yet offering an irresistible trophy. Without pausing to think it through, she moved towards him, standing in front of him with the challenge sparkling in her eyes.

'Not scared,' she said. 'Not of you.'

She had taken him by surprise; she could see that in his fleeting change of expression. He sat there for whole seconds looking up at her, the grey eyes acquiring a narrowed intensity. When he reached for her it was with an air almost of resignation, as if he had fought a battle within himself and lost.

Last time he had kissed her it had been in anger and without compunction. This time held a kind of anger too, but of a totally different kind. Claire found herself responding to it, needing it almost. She buried her hands in the thickness of his hair, nearly losing sight of the object of the exercise in the sudden surging heat of the moment. She had never known anything like this before; he made Peter seem like an immature youth. She wanted it to go on for ever.

The touch of his fingers on her breast made her arch. He handled her with knowledge and expertise, his every caress driving her further and further away from control. She was conscious of textures against her bare skin, the softness of his shirt, the hardness of his buttons. Then the shirt was gone and the textures had changed, soft and hard in another context. It took every ounce of her will to stop him undressing her completely. She wanted him to, heaven only knew, but not here like this. What had begun as a means of revenge had backfired on her.

'No,' she whispered desperately when he carried right on. 'Rod, I can't!'

'Yes, you can.' His voice was rough, his hands unrelenting. 'You're not backing out on me now!'

'What about my father?' she asked. 'He trusted you, Rod!'

He went suddenly still, his whole body tensed. Then abruptly he thrust himself up and away from her, reaching for the shirt he had so recently discarded. His face was tight, his anger held in check with an obvious effort.

'I ought to damned well make you come through anyway,' he said between his teeth. 'You'd got it all worked out, hadn't you!'

'Not that far,' she admitted ashamedly. 'I never intended to let it get that far.'

'Oh, I see. A couple of kisses just to warm me up, then a quick withdrawal leaving me yearning for more. You remember what you got last time you tried that game on with me?' He didn't wait for an answer, flicking a brief searing glance over her. 'Waste of time and effort where you're concerned. Just think yourself lucky you've got Bill behind you!'

Claire buttoned her own shirt with unsteady fingers, knowing she deserved every word. 'I'm sorry,' she said. 'I really am sorry. If it means anything at all, I never had that much trouble holding back before.'

He looked at her with cynicism. 'Then why bother?'

'Because it's meaningless without any other emotion involved.'

'Such as your fiancé can conjure?'

'My ... Oh, you mean Peter?'

'Who else?' There was irony in his voice. 'He is the man your father is trying to stop you from marrying, isn't he?'

'Yes.'

'Having second thoughts?'

Claire flushed in the dim light. 'I'm not sure the first ones were ever really so definite. There was a good chance I'd have cried off before the wedding.'

'Why?'

She hesitated, avoiding his eyes. 'Because I was marrying him for all the wrong reasons, I suppose. I don't love him.'

'You don't love anybody,' came the hard response. 'Unless it's yourself.'

'That's not true!' She swallowed hard on the lump in her throat. 'I discovered on the plane coming out here how much Bill means to me. When you think someone might be dead or dying nothing else matters.'

'You soon changed your tune when you realised how he'd tricked you.'

'On the surface, perhaps. Not underneath. I was angry because he'd put me in this position, but I didn't hate him for it.'

'Not the way you hated me.'

She glanced at him then, sensing ridicule, but the grey eyes were level. 'No,' she admitted, 'not the way I hated you. You went out of your way to make me.'

'You could be right. You needed a shock and I saw myself providing it.' He paused and shrugged. 'I didn't intend letting things get to the point they got to tonight either. Good thing you called a halt—I'd never have felt able to look your father in the eye again.'

Something in her prompted the soft comment, 'You recover fast from frustration.'

His shrug was light. 'Like you said, there was no emotion involved. That's when it really reckons.'

'Has it ever?' she asked because she couldn't help herself. 'Reckoned, I mean.'

The grey eyes flickered. 'If it had it wouldn't be a subject I'd be ready to talk about.' He came to his feet, lean and lithe and very male, tucking the free ends of his shirt back into his jeans. 'Shall I be telling the truth if I get a cable off to Bill in the morning to the effect that you've changed you mind about marrying St John?'

Claire sighed. 'Yes. I suppose you'll be glad to have me off your hands.'

'I'd as soon the temptation were removed, yes,' he came back dryly. 'For everybody, not just me. I wouldn't like to hazard a guess at Loxley's frame of mind, but his concentration's been suffering this last day or two. I'll try and arrange transport back to Dar for Tuesday. Till then, steer clear of him, will you?'

Claire nodded, not trusting herself to speak. She felt mixed up. With the door closed behind him she sat trying to sort herself out. Two more days and she would be on her way home. That was what she had wanted, wasn't it, so why this lack of feeling? The truth stared her in the face, despite all she could do to hide from it. She didn't want to go, not any more. Life had purpose here on camp. Back home lay the same old routine. She would have to take steps to change it, that was for sure. Somehow or other she had to find herself a job.

She knew there was more to it than that. She didn't want to go because Rod was staying. Lack of emotional involvement had been a lie on her part. The only thing stopping her had been *his* lack of it. Given a little time she might be able to do something about changing his attitude, but not in two days. At least, not enough. And it would be weeks before he was back in England.

It wasn't difficult to avoid Derek Loxley next day as he spent most of it on the work site. Apart from a few minutes at midday when he informed her that a plane would be out from the coast to fetch her the following morning, she saw nothing of Rod either. It was as if nothing had happened between them. Certainly when he looked at her there was no flicker of feeling there in his eyes.

By evening she was desperate enough to go looking for him, finding him eventually in the company of the site foreman.

'I'm going back out to the site to check some figures,' he said when she asked if she could speak to him privately. 'You'd better come with me if it's so urgent.' He ignored the other man's sly grin, gathering up the graphs they had been working on. 'Ready?'

They were in one of the jeeps and heading along the track before he spoke again.

'You're not helping matters, are you?' he said brusquely. 'I've kept out of your way with a purpose today.'

Claire directed an oblique glance which told her nothing beyond the fact that he was good and angry. 'You don't want me to go,' she said, 'any more than I want to go.'

It was a moment before he answered. When he did speak it was on a distinctly discouraging note. 'Don't let's get things out of perspective. What happened last night was strictly off the cuff.'

'What nearly happened last night,' Claire corrected. She hesitated, then forced herself on. 'If it had would you have felt any differently?'

'About keeping you here?' His smile was grim. 'It's a debatable point.'

'I didn't mean that. I meant about me—personally.'

They had reached the darkened site. Rod brought the vehicle to a standstill outside the site office and switched off the ignition before turning his head to look at her, expression unrevealing. 'Different in what way?'

'Would it have meant anything to you?'

He laughed shortly. 'I thought we agreed there was nothing like that involved.'

'I ... changed my mind.'

The silence was brief but infused. He eyed her narrowly. 'What's that supposed to mean?'

'I just want to be with you. I don't care in what capacity, just so long as I don't have to get on that plane in the morning!'

'Let me get this straight,' he said. 'You're offering to stay on here and be whatever I ask you to be. Right?'

'Yes.'

His mouth thinned. 'Does that include sleeping with me?'

'If you want me to.' She refused to drop her eyes from his. 'Bill always said that anything worth having is worth going out on a limb for.' She drew in a breath, knowing she was probably doing this all wrong, yet unable to see any other way in the time she had left. 'Rod, don't you see? This is what he planned on happening. He didn't like my choice in men so he sent me out to one he knew could make me forget him, given half a chance. Well, it worked. I have forgotten Peter. Compared with you, he's nothing!' She slid a hand beseechingly along his sleeve up to his shoulder, feeling the muscle tense beneath her fingers. 'Don't just sit there looking at me like that. Kiss me!'

Rod did so like a man in a dream, almost as if he couldn't help himself. Claire clung to him, responding with lips and heart, exultant in her triumph. When they finally drew apart she was laughing and breathless, eyes luminous in the starlight.

'You see, we do both feel the same. Oh, Rod, it's going

to be wonderful! I'll stay on here at Mgala till you bring in this job, then we can travel home together, Bill's going to be delighted!'

The lean features wore an odd expression. 'Think so?'

'I'm sure so. You're exactly the kind of son-in-law he'd want. He'll probably make you a partner. Naughton and Gilvray. It sounds ...' She broke off in sudden disconcertion. 'What is it? What have I said?'

He was laughing himself, leaning back in his seat to regard her with a wondering shake of his head. 'Claire, you're fantastic. You really are! Just when did you decide I was husband material?'

'Last night after you'd gone. At least, that was when I realised how I felt about you.'

'And the rest automatically followed?'

'Not automatically, no. I had to be sure you felt the same way first.'

'Isn't one kiss rather weak evidence?'

'Not the way you just kissed me.' She was beginning to suspect his reactions. She tagged on swiftly. 'If I took too much for granted ...'

'That's one way of putting it.' The amusement was still there, curling about his lips. 'One minute I seem set to get myself a bed partner, the next I'm halfway down the aisle! For surprise strategy that takes some beating.'

'I meant it,' she said. 'I do want to marry you, Rod.'

'Oh, sure you do. The same way you wanted to marry St John.'

'That was a mistake. I already explained.' Claire put her hand on his sleeve again, this time leaving it where it was. 'I've changed. I know what I really want now.'

'That's nice. Pity you're not going to get it.' He shook his head at the look on her face, smile dry. 'It's a tempting offer, darling, but I'll have to turn it down. If and when

I take myself a wife it's going to be my choice, not just hers.'

'But I love you!' she said desperately.

'I doubt it. Even if you did it doesn't put me under any obligation. One thing you still have to realise is you can't have everything you want just by saying it.' He swung out a leg. 'Just sit tight while I find what I came for.'

Claire did exactly that. Every nerve in her body was stretched to its limit. She had made a complete fool of herself, and to what purpose? Rod didn't care about her. Not the way she wanted him to care.

Staring out at the dark bulk of machinery scattered about the site, she felt a sudden surging need to make some gesture—a metaphorical if not physical thumbing of the nose at the man who had turned her down. There were no lights on the site because the generators weren't working. Apart from the flickering beam of the torch Rod had brought with him and which he was now using in the office, the only illumination came from the jeep headlights pointing directly towards the dirt road coming in from the mine and town. She could reach the latter long before he could find some more transport and follow her.

What she was going to do when she got there seemed immaterial at the moment. She slid over into the driving seat without stopping to consider anything beyond getting the jeep into motion. Four-wheel-drive wasn't new to her, although the Range Rover she had tried had been vastly more refined than this battered relic. She set off with a clashing of gears which brought Rod out of the office in double quick time, smiling in satisfaction as the torch beam fell astern in the rear view mirror. He had a half mile walk back to camp. She hoped he enjoyed it.

The satisfaction didn't last long. Before she had gone a mile she was bitterly regretting the impulse. What good was it going to do? She couldn't force Rod into returning her feelings. On the contrary, she was likely to have alienated him totally with this stunt of hers.

She thought about turning back, but didn't feel capable of executing a turn in the dark without running off the road in the process, and wasn't sure enough of the terrain either side of it to run the risk. She would just have to keep going until she reached town and then decide on a course of action.

Fool! she thought fiercely. All this for a man! But the ache deep inside her wouldn't go. Rod wasn't just any man, he was the one man who had ever managed to make any real impression on her emotions. She wanted him with everything in her, not just physically but wholly and completely. And she couldn't have him, he had made that clear.

Journey's end came sooner than she had anticipated when the fuel tank ran dry. Sitting there in the thick darkness she could sense the vastness around her. The stars had vanished, obliterated by cloud. All she needed now was for it to rain and her cup would literally be flowing over.

It came some few minutes later, the heavens opening in a downpour which soaked her to the skin in seconds. There wasn't even a canvas roof to this particular vehicle. All she could do was huddle miserably down into her seat and wait for the rain to cease. She could hardly get any wetter.

It had slackened a little but not stopped when she heard the faint sound of an engine approaching. The headlights found her shortly after, the other car drawing to a stop with its front bumper right up to her rear. Rod had brought the Land-Rover, Claire noted. That meant he at least would be warm and dry. She got out before he could move, and splashed back through the mud and gravel to squelch into the seat beside him, steeling herself for the inevitable.

'I ran out of fuel,' she said.

'You ran out of a great deal more,' he responded on a grim note. 'Like common sense, for instance. What was this supposed to prove?'

'Not a thing,' she admitted wearily. 'It was a stupid thing to do.' She tried to stop shivering, smoothing back the sodden hair from her face with a hand that trembled. 'Do you think you'll be able to get round in this?'

'I can only try.' Whatever else he had to say he was obviously saving it for a more convenient moment. 'It's going to be sticky.'

It was more than that, it was impossible. He let go with a curse as the rear wheels slid off relatively firm ground and sank into mud. 'That does it,' he said. 'No use trying to push us out in this. We'll have to wait till it stops.'

'How long is that likely to be?' Claire's teeth were chattering now, not so much with cold as sheer nervous reaction. 'Does it usually go on all night?'

'Not often at this time of year, although the rainy seasons are getting to be as erratic as the rest of the world's weather from all accounts.' He made a sudden move, leaning over his seat to fish up what appeared to be a blanket from the floor in the rear of the car. 'Get in the back and get those wet things off. This won't be very clean, but it's the best on offer.'

Claire did as she was told without argument. Clean or not, the dry blanket felt warm and comforting to her skin. When she turned her head to the front it was to meet Rod's eyes in the driving mirror. In the darkness he could have seen little of her but the flash of paler flesh as she moved, yet that in itself was enough to bring a warmth to her cheeks.

'You were watching,' she accused.

He inclined his head without bothering to look round at her. 'Considering the offer you made me some time back I felt entitled. Don't worry, you were just a shape. The only curves I saw were in my mind's eye.'

'Louse,' she said bitterly. 'Last night was different.'

'You don't need to tell me that. You weren't looking like a drowned rat, for one thing. I hope you've been taking your paludrine regularly,' he added. 'This isn't a malarial area broadly speaking, but you never know what this lot might bring out in the way of livestock.' He did glance round at her when she failed to answer, eyes probing the gloom to asses her expression. 'Have you?'

'I didn't bring any.' Her tone was defensive. 'I'd already had the typhoid and yellow fever jabs because Peter planned to visit Kenya on our ... honeymoon. I didn't think anything else was necessary.'

Looking into the reflected glow from the headlights, she could see his jaw clench. Without speaking, he put a hand into one of the dashboard compartments and came away with a flat tin. The tablets he gave her were pale and round.

'Take them,' he said. 'And keep on taking them till well after you're home and dry. Malaria's no joke.'

'None of this is a joke,' she responded on a flat intonation, swallowing the tablets. 'Not to me. I never threw myself at anyone's head before.'

'Put it down to experience,' came the unmoved response. 'It could have been worse.'

'You mean if you'd made love to me and *then* turned me down.'

His mouth slanted. 'The way you approached the subject it could easily have happened.'

Her next question was a long time coming. 'Could it still?' She saw his sharp movement and added swiftly. 'I'm not just asking for the sake of it. I need to know. Did I turn you off altogether?'

His reply was an even longer time coming. He just sat there looking at her. Finally he sighed and shook his head.

'Apparently not. Having you take your things off wasn't such a good idea.'

'Make love to me,' she whispered. 'Please, Rod.'

His jaw had tensed. 'Claire, for God's sake!'

'I want you to. I don't care about anything else right now!'

'You would tomorrow.'

'I don't care about that either.' She slid the blanket from her shoulders, kneeling there in the folds of it, her drying hair falling about her face in a dark cloud. 'Forget what I said earlier—I was being foolish. I just want you to make love to me.'

He made a sound like a groan and came through between the two seats, dropping to his knees to pull her to him. She kissed him back feverishly, quivering to the feel of his hands moving over her body, needing a swift arousal to overcome the doubts still there in her mind. When he spread the blanket and laid her on it she went down without protest, hearing the drumming of the rain on the roof above like some distant thunder almost drowned by that in her ears. I love him, she told herself in fierce defence against her father's image. I love him!

It was Rod himself who called a halt, lifting his head to look at her with some new expression dawning in his face. 'This really is the first time for you, isn't it?' he said.

She was trembling with a mixture of anticipation and faint apprehension, her whole body poised on the brink of discovery. The eyes looking back at him were glazed, not understanding. 'Yes,' she whispered.

His teeth came together hard enough to make her wince involuntarily, then he was rolling away from her, sitting up to run a hand forcefully through his hair before coming to rest with both forearms resting on his bent knees.

'Get dressed,' he said. His voice sounded rough.

'I can't. They're still wet.' Claire was almost in tears,

unable to take in the sudden change in him. 'Rod, I ...'

'Then put the damned blanket round you,' he gritted.

She did so with difficulty, huddling into it with a choking misery clogging her throat. 'I'm sorry,' she got out. 'I didn't realise it would make a difference.'

'It makes a difference.' His tone was savage. 'I never took a virgin in my life, and I'm damned if I'm going to start with Bill Naughton's daughter!'

It was all she could do to say it. 'You didn't believe me, then, when I told you I didn't sleep around.'

'Sure I believed you. That didn't have to mean you hadn't been with any man before. St John, for instance—assuming he's capable.'

'I'm quite sure he's capable. Being engaged to him didn't mean I had to go to bed with him, did it?' She made an effort to bring herself under control. 'How did you know, anyway?'

'I knew, that's enough.' He stirred. 'The rain's stopping. I'm going to get us out of here.'

'Rod, don't be like this,' she pleaded. 'You're making me feel like a tramp!'

'You can hardly be that, considering.' He turned his head to look at her, mouth still tight. 'Why me, Claire? Why do me the honour?'

'I told you,' she said huskily. 'I love you. You turned down the idea of marriage, so I decided to take what was left. Is that so unusual?'

'Where you're concerned nothing should surprise me any more,' he retorted without any appreciable softening. 'You're no more in love with me than you were with St John. You just can't take being on the receiving end. It wouldn't matter what it cost you if you thought there was a chance of coming out on top.'

It hadn't been like that, but there was little point in denying it. He simply wasn't going to believe her. She bit hard on her lower lip as he got to his feet.

'You're going to have to take the wheel while I push from behind,' he said brusquely. 'Not too much throttle or she'll just churn up the mud. Start her up when I yell.'

Claire waited until he was out of the vehicle before moving forward to slide behind the wheel, tucking the blanket securely across the top of her breasts sarong fashion. It took two attempts to free the rear end from its muddy resting place and get it back on the harder surface of the road. When Rod climbed in again he was sodden to the knees.

He didn't say a word on the way back to camp. The sky had begun to clear, allowing a star or two to twinkle through. There was a pungent smell of wet earth and vegetation in the air. Had it been daylight the ground would already have been steaming in the undiminished heat of the sun.

Had it been daylight none of this would have happened, Claire thought numbly. It took darkness to release inhibitions the way hers had been released. If Rod had made love to her back there she would at least have had something worth remembering. This way she had nothing.

There was little sign of activity when they finally made camp. The rain had obviously kept everyone indoors. Rod drove the car as close to her door as he could, leaving the engine idling.

'A hot shower wouldn't hurt if you feel like making the effort,' he said. 'There's nobody over there right now.'

Claire shook her head. 'I'll wait till morning when the mud's dried out a little.' She paused, fighting for a calm note. 'What time will my plane be here?'

'Around eleven. There's a flight out of Dar early evening.' He didn't add, 'be on it', but his tone implied it. The latter changed abruptly. 'I'm sorry about what happened back there. I should have had more sense.'

'It was my fault . . .' she began, but he cut her off.

'No, it was mine. Last night was one mistake, tonight an even bigger one.'

'Except that you didn't make it.' She thought about the morning and felt desperation sweep over her. 'Rod, it wasn't like you think. I wasn't trying to put you under any obligation. You're the only man I ever felt this way about! If I can't have you, I don't want anybody!'

He shook his head in sudden impatience. 'You just never give up, do you? All right, supposing I agreed to everything you've suggested tonight. How long do you think it would last?' He gave her no chance to answer. 'I'll tell you how long. Till the novelty wore off. You only want what you haven't got, and once you get it there's no interest left. Thanks, but no, thanks. You go and find yourself some other quarry to bring down.'

'If you'd let me stay I could prove you wrong in this instance,' she said, grasping at the slender thread of hope his words appeared to provide. 'All that might have been true once, but not where you're concerned. I'll do whatever you say, if you'll just cancel that plane tomorrow. No strings attached. All I'm asking for is the chance to make you feel the same way I feel about you.'

He was silent for what seemed an age, eyes searching her face framed within its cloud of dark hair, dropping to the bare gleam of her shoulders above the blanket. She saw the contraction about his mouth and knew he wanted her again. She seized advantage of the moment to slide along the seat and put her arms about his neck, pressing her lips to his with pleading. 'Please, Rod!'

His voice was low. 'What would you tell your father?'

'Anything. It doesn't matter.' The scent of victory lifted her head, sparkling the green eyes like twin emeralds. 'On the face of it I'll only be doing what he wanted.'

'He'd discover the truth soon enough. We couldn't keep it quiet in a set-up like this.'

'I'm of age,' she defended. 'I'm free to make my own decisions.'

'And that's as much as you care, isn't it?' He put up his hands and seized both her wrists in a painfully hard grip, dragging them down from about his neck. 'You don't give a damn who gets hurt just so long as little Claire gets her own way! Well, you're not doing it with me, sweetheart. You'll be on that plane in the morning if I have to put you on it myself!'

Claire didn't move. 'You led me into that,' she said. 'You deliberately led me in!'

'That's right, I did. I needed to know just how far you were prepared to go. You haven't changed, Claire. You couldn't care less about Bill. Bringing me home in tow would be an ideal way of getting back at him for sending you out here in the first place, wouldn't it? An ideal way of getting back at me too, if it comes to that. Nobody gets the better of Claire Naughton!' He paused, the skin around his mouth stretched tight. 'Are you going to get out, or do I come round there and fetch you out?'

She opened the door without another word and stepped down to the ground, bare feet sinking into mud. There was no one around to witness her stumbling progress across the intervening space between car and hut; she doubted if she would have cared very much had there been. She heard the Land-Rover move off as she closed the door behind her.

Was it true? she wondered achingly. Was she really the kind of person Rod had described? If she was, why did she feel this terrible hurt over the things he had said? And why, in spite of all of it, did she still so desperately want him?

CHAPTER FIVE

MORNING found her hollow-eyed and weary after an all but sleepless night. She waited until she was certain that the last of the men would have cleared the shower house before making the effort to drag herself across, dressing afterwards in the same linen suit in which she had arrived just a week ago.

It was gone eight-thirty by the time she finished. Not feeling like eating, she decided to go back to her room and wait. It would be Rod who took her out to the plane, if only to make sure she got on it. She dreaded seeing him again, yet longed for it too. Even if there was no chance of changing his mind, she could perhaps convince him that her motives had not been all he had imagined.

He came for her at ten-fifteen, driving one of the covered jeeps. The grey eyes were like those of a stranger, cool and remote.

'The plane will be here in a few minutes,' he said, hoisting her suitcase. 'The pilot wants to do a quick turn round, so we'd better be out there waiting for him. Have you got everything?'

Claire nodded, hardly trusting her voice. Only when they were outside and in the car did she say tentatively, 'Aren't I going to be allowed to say goodbye to anybody?'

'Loxley's out at the site,' came the curt response. 'I'll tell him for you.'

The plane was already visible as a distant speck in the sky to the east as they bumped along the rough track out to the airstrip. Under the baking sun, last night's mud was almost a memory, the acacia trees fringing the track as dry and arid-looking as they had ever been. Further west beyond the town the terrain became softer, with the agricultural scope her father had spoken of, but this was the Africa she would remember—scrub and dust. It echoed the emptiness inside her.

'Another minute,' Rod assessed with an eye on the growing shape in the sky as he brought the vehicle to a standstill on the edge of the strip. 'Good timing.' He sat with a forearm resting across the wheel looking out to the heat-hazed horizon, the coating of hair not so much darker than the tan of the skin beneath.

Claire put the tip of her tongue to lips gone dry, said on a husky note, 'Rod, couldn't we start all over again? Not here—I mean when you come back to England.'

He sighed without turning his head towards her. 'Can't you bear to just let it go? There's no future in it, for either of us.'

'There might be if we worked at it. You can't deny the attraction.'

His lips twisted. 'No,' he said, 'I can't deny the attraction. If it's any consolation, I could make a meal of you right here and now.' He looked at her then, glance sliding the length of her body with open regret. 'I keep seeing you the way you looked last night stretched out on that blanket, and kicking myself for not taking advantage of it. I must have been mad.'

Claire winced. 'All right,' she said low-toned, 'I deserved that. But do you think I could really have been as shameless about it if I didn't feel anything for you? If what you said about me was true I'd have hit on the idea a long time ago.'

'You never needed to go that far before,' he came back, unimpressed. 'Beyond a certain point you're as innocent as a babe.'

'Is that how you knew? Because I didn't do the things you're used to having a woman do?'

'You didn't do anything,' he said. 'That's how I knew. You just lay there like a lovely doll waiting for me to do it all. Not your fault if you've never been shown how.'

The plane was circling the strip prior to landing. Claire said softly. 'You could show me, Rod. I'd learn fast. Send the plane away again and take me back with you. Please!'

He drew in a hard breath. 'How many times do I have to say it? You're not staying!'

'Then promise me you'll come and see me as soon as you get back to England.'

'I'll think about it.' He got out of the jeep, reaching for her suitcase, face closed against any further entreaty. 'Come on, I want you on that plane.'

The Cessna came to a stop some twenty yards away from where they stood. Rod walked her out to it, a hand under her arm as if even now he suspected she might try to make a break for it. The pilot was a younger man than the one who had brought her out. He jumped down to the grass as they approached, stretching both arms then easing the small of his back.

'That seat needs re-padding,' he commented wryly. 'Feel's like cast-iron.' He looked at Claire with interest. 'They didn't tell me who I was picking up. Not very often I get to fly a girl out from Mgala.'

'It won't be happening again,' Rod told him. 'This was a strictly one-off. How's the weather on the coast?'

'Humid,' came the answer, accompanied by a grimace. 'It's hotter here but still better for working in.' He glanced at his watch. 'We'll have to get moving. I've a schedule to meet.'

Claire watched her case stowed away in the rear, and allowed herself to be helped into her seat by a pair of impersonal hands. Only then, as she looked into the tanned features, did her resolve weaken.

'Rod?' she said pleadingly.

His expression didn't alter. 'I said I'd think about it.' He closed the door and lifted a hand to the man at her side. 'Take her away.'

Taxiing into position, the pilot said conversationally, 'That's a strong-willed man back there. If any girl looked at me the way you just looked at him, I'd be putty in her hands!'

The jeep was already on its way back to camp. Claire knew Rod would not be glancing back. She fixed her eyes on the markers beginning to flow towards them, wondering how she was going to get through the weeks before she saw him again. He would come. He had to come. If he didn't she would go looking for him.

She realised suddenly that the pilot had spoken. Her face turned towards him, unseeing. 'I'm sorry. What did you say?'

Smile dry, he shook his head. 'Forget it.'

Claire was already booked on the flight out from Dar es Salaam, she found when she went to check available seats. Rod had thought of everything. She toyed with the idea of cancelling and staying on here at the coast for a time, but had to concede that it would be pointless to do so. Nothing short of an emergency was going to get Rod away from Mgala before the job was completed, and he was far too wily to fall for any trick such as the one her father had played on her.

She could think of it now without anger, even with understanding. Without that interference she would have been marrying Peter less than a week from now. She still had the latter to face, of course, but that shouldn't prove too much of a problem. His own family hadn't been too keen on the match either. What Peter needed was someone who would give him a sense of purpose—as Rod had done for her. He was the one she was going to marry, come hell or high water. She didn't care how long it took to persuade him.

Bill was waiting at the airport when she landed at eight. His greeting was a little tentative as if he still weren't certain which way she might jump. Claire took a tongue-in-cheek delight in keeping him guessing for a while.

'I checked the passenger list,' he said when she asked him in the car how he had been so sure she would be on the flight. 'Rod's cable only said probably.'

'He should have had more faith,' Claire returned lightly. 'Or perhaps he just knows me too well. I almost stayed on in Dar es Salaam. I would have done if there'd been any chance of getting him there.'

Her father gave her a swift glance. 'Does that mean what I think it means?'

'It means,' she said, 'that I'm going to marry Rod Gilvray. Surprised?'

He certainly looked all of that. But not disapproving, she noted. She added softly, 'Isn't that what you hoped for?'

'It had crossed my mind,' he admitted on a bemused note. 'But not so soon.' He smiled a little. 'I'd have thought even you might have difficulty persuading Rod Gilvray to give up his freedom.'

'I am, but it isn't insurmountable.' Claire wished she felt as certain as she sounded. 'Do you have any job lined up for him when he gets back to England?'

'Yes, I do. We got the contract for the Colwood Valley dam. Rod already saw the specification.'

Relief filled her. 'So he'll be staying in the country for some time.'

'Eighteen months.' There was confusion now in her

father's voice. 'Just let me get this straight. Rod hasn't actually asked you to marry him yet?'

'No, I asked him.' She kept her tone level. 'He refused.'

'Did he?' He gave her a swift speculative glance. 'Obviously not with enough conviction to dampen your hopes. Think he's playing hard to get?'

'No,' she said again. 'He doesn't trust me. He thinks it's impossible for me to have fallen out of love with Peter and in love with him all in the space of a week.'

'Can't say I blame him too much for that. It does seem a bit quick.'

'Except that I was never in love with Peter in the first place. Not in any way that really counted.'

'You were going to marry him.'

'I know, and I'm ashamed of it.' She paused. 'How did he take it?'

'Not very well. You're going to have to sort things out with him yourself, I'm afraid.' It was Bill's turn to pause. 'I take it I'm forgiven for putting in my oar the way I did.'

'For what you did, yes. I'm not so sure about the way you did it.'

'Did it ... matter to you?'

Claire turned her head then to look at him, seeing the uncertainty in his eyes with a sudden rush of emotion. Impulsively she put out a hand and covered his large brown one. 'Yes, it mattered. A great deal.'

His smile held a new warmth. 'I'm sorry, but there didn't seem any other way. I knew I could rely on Rod not to let me down once you were safely out at Mgala.' He caught the change in her expression and his own altered too, the smile fading a little. 'Claire,' he added hesitantly, 'you and Rod ...'

'I haven't been to bed with him, if that's what you're thinking,' she came in candidly. 'Not that I wouldn't have

done if he'd been willing. Being your daughter puts me
outside that kind of relationship in his book. He has too
much of a regard for you.'

'I'm glad to hear it.' He seemed to be unsure whether
she was teasing him or not. 'Did you make him that offer
too?'

She smiled wryly. 'If you want the truth, I threw myself
quite shamelessly at his head. He could have had anything he wanted, with or without marriage thrown in.'

There was more wonder than censure in the eyes looking back at her. 'I've never known you like this before,'
her father said.

'I've never felt like this before,' she admitted. 'Isn't it
the way Mother felt about you?'

'If it was she made sure I never knew it,' came the dry
return. 'It says a whole lot for Rod if he managed to turn
down *that* kind of offer—unless you simply leave him cold.'

'I don't!' It was said with emphasis. 'He wants me.'

'But not enough to marry you.'

'He will. He'll have to!' Claire turned appealing eyes on
her father. 'Couldn't you offer him a partnership or something?'

'You mean by way of a bribe?'

'I suppose so.'

'Would you want him that way?'

'I want him any way I can get him,' she said fiercely.
'I don't care how! I love him.'

Bill shook his head. 'That isn't love, it's obsession.' His
tone had gone flat. 'You were always the same as a child.
Deny you anything, no matter how small, and that was the
one thing you had to have.'

'This is different. *I'm* different!'

'Are you? I wonder.' Studying her, he softened again.
'Claire, be sensible. Rod Gilvray isn't the kind of man
you can wind round your little finger. If he says he won't

marry you then it's odds on that he won't, no matter what the incentive.'

A tremor ran through her. 'You mean you won't help me?'

He sighed. 'I won't offer him any partnership on the grounds you're suggesting, no.' He leaned forward to tap on the closed screen between front and rear of the vehicle, barely waiting until the driver had slid it back to say brusquely, 'Stop at the Crown. I need a drink.'

Claire was motionless for a moment or two after he had sat back again. When she spoke at least it was with shamed apology. 'You're right, I was going too far. I have to do it myself.'

'Good girl!' He sounded relieved. 'I thought you'd see it that way in the end. If Rod did join the family I'd be more than happy, of course, but I wouldn't want a son-in-law who allowed himself to be bought.'

'It wouldn't have worked anyway. He has too much pride.' She paused. 'There is one thing you could do, though.'

'What's that?' cautiously.

'Get him out to the house when he comes home—even if it means arranging some special weekend party or something.'

'You really think a weekend is going to be long enough?'

'It would be a start.'

'Well, you know best about that.' He still sounded doubtful. 'I'll do what I can.'

And in the meantime she must wait with what patience she could muster, Claire acknowledged, and knew that no weeks were ever going to seem as long again as the ones coming.

Straightening matters out with Peter proved to be more of an ordeal than she had anticipated. They parted eventually on less than amicable terms with little chance of attaining mutual understanding at any time in the foreseeable future. Claire was sorry to have lost Peter's friendship, but unswerving in her new resolve. From now on, no one mattered but Rod. She longed for him with everything in her. Had she been able to write to him it might have helped to relieve her feelings, but contact of any kind was not part of her plans. When they met again he had to see her in a totally new light.

It was partly towards this end that she started a course in business studies which took up the greater part of the working week. The realisation after the first week that she was beginning to find a real interest in what she was doing came as a bonus which took her by surprise. Bill teased her about the whole thing, yet was obviously pleased about it too. 'We'll have you on the exec staff before we know where we are,' he joked on one occasion, to which Claire smiling replied that nothing less than his own job would satisfy her.

She formed new friendships too, one of which could have proved more meaningful than most had her heart and mind been free. Blake Wrexham was taking an advanced course in economics which covered more or less the same hours as her own. They formed the habit of taking lunch together, and on one or two occasions stayed on in town to take in a theatre or dinner. Blake was twenty-seven and ambitious—a man who knew what he wanted from life. Claire found herself telling him about Rod, and received sympathetic if somewhat wry encouragement.

'I wish I could comand the same devotion,' he said. 'I doubt if I'd need twice asking!'

Claire smiled at him across the table for two, liking the way his fair hair fell across his clever, high-browed forehead—liking him. 'I suppose I should have more pride than to run after a man who needs persuading.'

'Why?' he came back. 'If he's what you want, go get him. I admire that kind of spirit.' His smile held a touch of regret. 'I might even give him a run for his money if I had the time. I could do with a little loving.'

'But not enough to fight for it?' she suggested, not taking him at all seriously. 'Shame on you, Blake!'

'A case of priorities right now,' he agreed, not in the least abashed. 'If you change your mind about this engineer, I'll still be around.'

Claire hadn't changed her mind when the time came for Rod to return home to England, but after a week had gone by without any attempt at contact on his part it became obvious that any move was going to have to be made by her.

Bill shrugged philosophically when she reminded him about the weekend party she had suggested.

'You can try it, if you like. Who else did you think of inviting?'

Claire told him with some slight diffidence, aware of his lack of enthusiasm. 'You don't think it's going to be any good, do you?' she asked, and he shook his head.

'No, I don't. If Rod had wanted to get in touch with you he'd have done it under his own steam.'

'And you don't like the thought of any daughter of yours sinking so low as to run after a man?' She saw his expression and knew she had hit the nail on the head. She added despairingly, 'I love him. Doesn't that make a difference?'

'Not if he doesn't love you. You can't force a man into feeling something he doesn't want to feel.'

'Can't you?' Her tone was stubborn. 'One can but try.'

Regardless of what she had said to her father, Claire decided to let the invitation to spend the weekend at the Naughton home be the deciding factor. If Rod refused on any grounds whatsoever, she would take it as proof that he wanted nothing more to do with her, although accepting that it would tear the heart out of her.

She was on tenterhooks until she saw Bill the following night, her eyes asking the question almost before he was inside the house.

'He accepted,' he said. Without looking directly at her, he added, 'There's just one snag—he asked if he could bring someone with him. I could hardly say no.'

Claire had gone very still. 'A girl?' she got out.

'Yes. And not just any girl either. Pauline Barton. She's a top buyer at Harrods. Apparently he's known her some time. Very well, by all accounts.' There was a weary compassion in his glance. 'Claire, forget him. He isn't the kind to settle for one while he can still play the field. He'll only bring you heartache.'

'I don't care.' She did, but there was no way she was going to show defeat now. 'What's a little competition!'

'More than a little. She's a very good-looking young woman.'

'You've met her?'

'I've seen her. They were in the same restaurant for lunch the other day.' The pause was brief. 'I hear tell he was living with her before he went out to Mgala.'

Claire's chin lifted fractionally. 'It's now I'm interested in.'

'In that case you don't have to worry too much. He's still in a hotel. Not much point in looking for a flat when he's due to move north inside a month.'

'So soon?' She was dismayed. 'I thought that job wasn't due to start until September.'

'It's been brought forward. You should be glad. At least he'll be out of this Pauline Barton's clutches.'

There was that, Claire agreed mentally, wondering what the job situation was like in the north. It was a big project they were going to be on up there. Perhaps there might even be something for her on site. She was becoming quite a competent typist, and her book-keeping passed muster as far as they had gone. Some practical experience could only stand her in good stead.

Rod and his companion were the last of the guests to arrive on the Saturday morning. Watching the possessive manner with which the tall, cool blonde took his arm as they entered the house, Claire knew the swift stab of jealousy. This woman knew Rod with an intimacy she herself did not, and she hated her for it. She was hard put not to let her emotions show on her face as she went to greet the pair.

Rod looked much the same as the first time she had set eyes on him, his casual jacket open over beige shirt and slacks. The grey eyes were steady as she performed the necessary introductions.

'The others are all in the drawing room,' said Claire. 'Would you like to join them? Lunch will be about half an hour.'

'That gives me time for a quick change into something a little less businesslike,' Pauline put in before Rod could respond. The smiling gesture she made disparaged the beautifully cut grey suit she was wearing while at the same time managing to draw attention to the way it fitted her willowy figure. 'I came straight from the office, as you might have guessed. You go ahead, Rod.'

He did just that, leaving Claire to show the other girl upstairs to the bedroom allocated her.

'Sorry it's a bit on the small side,' she proffered from the doorway. 'We don't very often use the singles, but it's full house this weekend.'

'It's charming,' Pauline assured her, looking anything but charmed. A little too casually, she added, 'Whereabouts is Rod?'

Claire took a somewhat malicious pleasure in telling her.

'Down at the far end of the gallery in the other single. I must remember to tell him before he comes up or he might think he's in his usual room.'

The blonde head turned sharply. 'He stays here often?'

'Whenever he's invited,' said Claire with strict truth. 'Can you find your own way down when you're ready? I'd better get back to the others.'

She meant Rod, and Pauline knew it. Her face was stiff with suspicion. Going downstairs again, Claire felt a pang of conscience, swiftly stifled. All was fair in love and war— and this was a little of both. Pauline wore no ring of Rod's to state prior claim. It was an open contract.

He was standing in a group consisting of her father and the Lattimers who were family friends of long standing, his back to the room. Claire took her time getting to him, aware of his eyes on her through the big gilt-framed mirror hanging over the fireplace as she moved among the other guests. There were eight in all, forming a mixed but she hoped complementary bag. Certainly everyone appeared to be getting along well enough.

Bill slid a fond parental arm about her shoulders when she finally reached him, drawing her into the circle.

'I was just telling them about your college course,' he said. 'Jerry's thinking about booking you for when his secretary retires next year.'

'At least I'd know he wasn't chasing some blonde bomb-shell around the office,' laughed Mary Lattimer.

'If I had the energy, I wouldn't have the time,' commented her husband dryly. 'It's all a myth. What exactly are you thinking of doing with you new-found talents, Claire?'

'I'm not sure,' she admitted. Her eyes met Rod's, the latter as unreadable as only he could make them. 'It depends on how well I do. I wouldn't mind travelling.'

'There's plenty of scope,' Rod agreed without any par-

ticular response to the innuendo. 'You'll need some practical experience first, though.'

'So I've been told.' This time she had scored; she could
see the faint glint spring in his eyes. 'I should be able to
find that within the Comany, don't you think?'

'If that's a hint that I should find you a job,' chuckled
her father, 'it's been taken heed of. How much longer do
you have to do?'

'Another three weeks on this present term. I could go
back for an advanced class in the autumn, if I found I
needed it.'

'You really are taking this seriously, aren't you?' Mary
Lattimer sounded surprised. 'I thought it was just a passing fancy.'

'Like all my others?' Claire said it without resentment.
'Not this time. I intend to put it to good use.'

Conversation became general after that, the two groups
merging into one. Seeing Rod move casually across to look
out of one of the tall windows at the gardens, Claire nerved
herself to follow him, only too well aware that Pauline
should be coming through the door any moment now.

'You can't see the best of it from here,' she said, moving
up beside him. 'It was rather badly planned in that respect.
I could show you the rose gardens if you're interested.'

He turned his head a little to look at her, a smile playing
faintly about his lips. 'You haven't altered,' he said.

Green eyes held grey for a long, meaningful moment.
'Not in one respect,' she agreed. 'Why haven't you been
before this, Rod?'

He shrugged lightly. 'Pressure of work.'

'You found time for—other things.'

'Other things,' he said with deliberation, 'don't have
strings attached.'

'And you think I do?'

'I know you do.' The smile was still there, but stiffer.

'Claire, don't start that all over again. I'm here because I like coming, no other reason.'

'You didn't have to bring your mistress to prove it!'

He didn't turn a hair. 'Pauline isn't here to prove anything. I happen to enjoy her company.'

'In bed?'

'And out of it.' He sighed suddenly. 'Look, I'm not going to spend the weekend swapping punchlines with you. I hoped you'd have come to your senses by now.'

'And stopped thinking about you that way?' Claire shook her head, mouth determined. 'I'm going to make you take me seriously, Rod. I really am. I don't care if I do have to compete with your blonde friend!'

His gaze moved over the oval of her face, lingered for a brief moment on the fullness of her mouth and took on a hint of self-mockery. 'It would hardly be a fair comparison.'

'To her or to me?'

'It all depends on the viewpoint.' His glance went beyond her, expression firming. 'Forget it, Claire. It's gone far enough.'

Not nearly as far as it was going to go, she vowed, turning her head to meet Pauline's narrowed gaze. Whatever happened, the other girl was not going to have him!

CHAPTER SIX

DETERMINATION was one thing, Claire was to find during that long afternoon, fulfilment quite another. Pauline stuck to Rod like a limpet, ignoring all gambits to remove her.

Changing for dinner, Claire had to acknowledge that the evening was likely to prove no more profitable. The only way she was going to have any time alone with Rod was by going to his room tonight after they had all retired. The attraction was still there; she could sense it in him. Making him want her again would be a step in the right direction.

Shameless, she thought wryly, and knew it was true. Where Rod was concerned, nothing else seemed to matter.

She deliberately chose a vibrant gold dress, suspecting that Pauline would plump for a classic black. Tight at the waist and softly moulded over her breasts, it looked satisfyingly eye-catching in the long dressing mirror. Her hair she swept into a swathe to one side of her head, allowing the length of it to drift over one shoulder.

Her father was already down and mixing cocktails, his thickset figure fined down by the dark dinner jacket.

'You look beautiful,' he said with approval. 'Diana the huntress!'

'Versus Helen of Troy.' She tried to keep her tone suitably light. 'Would you say it was true that most men prefer blondes?'

'Not this one,' he said. 'But then I'm biased.' He looked at her with a faint line drawn between his brows. 'Claire, why don't you just accept things the way they are? Rod brought Pauline along for a purpose.'

'He brought her for protection,' she returned with a lift of her head. 'If he hadn't wanted to see me again he'd have refused the invitation altogether. It's up to me to take him away from her.'

'You think you can?'

'I can but try.'

He hesitated, not quite meeting her eyes. 'I don't much care for the thought of my daughter having an affair with my top engineer.'

She laughed then, the sound brittle. 'Don't worry, neither does Rod.'

'He's hardly the marrying kind.'

'Is there such a thing? Surely it's a case of incentive. He once told me that the woman he married would have to be prepared to follow him wherever his job took him.'

'And you'd be prepared to do that?'

'Yes.' Her tone was soft. 'Oh yes!'

'Then you deserve to get him.' Smiling again, he handed her a glass. 'Good hunting!'

The others began arriving in dribs and drabs, over the following ten minutes or so. Rod and Pauline were the last down. They came in together, causing Claire to wonder painfully if their tawdriness was due to any joint distraction. The older girl looked coolly composed in the superbly styled black dress, but that wasn't to say she was cold underneath. No doubt she knew all there was to know about keeping a man happy in bed. It was she, Claire, who was the novice.

True to her prediction, she had little opportunity to speak with Rod all evening, although she caught his eyes on her once or twice and warmed to the appreciation in them. He looked devastating himself in the formal black and white. The longing to be in his arms again became overwhelming as the evening progressed.

It was almost two o'clock when the party finally broke

up, and another hour after that before the house was finally silent. Still wide awake, Claire slipped on a negligee and let herself cautiously out of her room, heart thudding like a trip-hammer. It seemed to take an age to traverse the length of the gallery, but she made it without mishap, drawing a steadying breath before turning the handle to slip inside the darkened room.

With the curtains partially opened, it was possible to see the reclining figure on the bed come swiftly up on an elbow.

'Pauline?' he asked low-toned but sharp. 'I thought we ...'

'It isn't Pauline, it's Claire,' she said, suddenly wishing she hadn't come. 'Don't put on the light, Rod.'

He made no attempt, lying there gazing across at her with expression obscured by the shadows. When he spoke again he sounded wary.

'So what's the next move? Am I supposed to drag you in here with me?'

'No,' she said. 'I just wanted to talk.'

'At three o'clock in the morning?'

'There hasn't been much chance tonight,' she defended. 'And your girlfriend will make sure there's no chance tomorrow either.'

'We don't have anything to talk about.'

'Yes, we do.' She took a small step forward, voice taking on a note of appeal. 'Rod, I know you're not indifferent to me, any more than I'm indifferent to you. Why can't you admit it?'

It was a moment before he answered. 'So I admit it. Short of making love to you, what am I supposed to do about it?'

'Get to know me better. Give me a chance to prove I'm not as shallow as you think I am.'

'To what end?'

'That has to depend on you. I just have to know I'm going to see you again after this weekend.'

It was possible to make out his features now as her eyes became accustomed to the darkness, but difficult to assess his expression. 'Didn't anyone ever tell you the male of the species is supposed to do the chasing?' he asked on an odd note.

'Yes, but you won't, so it has to be me.' She paused, watching him, wishing she could only read his thoughts. 'I don't give up easily.'

The smile was brief but encouraging. 'That I can vouch for!' He put out a hand, tone softening. 'Claire, come over here.'

She went without hesitation, sitting down on the edge of the mattress to look at him with a challenge in her eyes. 'If you're thinking of pulling an avuncular act, don't. I know what I'm doing. I love you, Rod. If you let me I can make you love me.'

The smile came again. 'Still the little egotist!'

'You can call me what you like, I don't care.' She lifted the hand she held to her breast, holding it there. 'You still want me, don't you?'

His breath was drawn in on a long audible note which suggested a certain resignation. 'Yes,' he said, 'I want you. I wanted you the first time I clapped eyes on you.' The fingers covering her curved to the shape of her, his other arm coming up to draw her to him. 'You're a witch, Claire. A lovely, self-centred, self-willed little witch!'

'Not for you,' she whispered. 'You're all I care about. Just love me, Rod. *Please* love me!'

There was constraint in the negative movement of his head. 'It wouldn't work out. Not the way you imagine.'

'You don't know what I imagine. You can't possibly know.' She put her lips to his jawline, kissing him with tiny, feather-light movements until she reached his mouth, sensing the response in him. His skin was slightly rough against hers, but it smelled so good—clean and tangy. He wasn't wearing a pyjama jacket and she could feel the hair on his chest through the flimsy material of her negligee as she pressed herself closer. Instinct guided her fingers across the muscular back to find the indentation of his spinal column and trace it slowly downwards, her pulses quickening to the growing raggedness of his breathing. This was what he had missed in her the last time. She had left it to him to do all the touching and caressing, intent only on her own pleasure. But there was pleasure in giving as well as in taking. She was just beginning to realise how much.

She felt deprived when he pushed her none too gently away from him, looking at him with eyes gone dark with hurt and bewilderment.

'Why?' she whispered. 'You want me, I *know* you want me!'

'You should do,' he came back grimly. 'You're doing your damnedest to make me. You don't give a hoot about anything, do you, sweetheart? You'd pull out all the stops to oust any hint of competition!'

'Where you're concerned, yes, I would,' she flashed. 'You only brought that woman with you to make me jealous! Well, I am jealous. I hate her for knowing you better than I do. I hate her because you've made love to her and you won't make it to me. 'I——' She broke off with a sudden hopeless little gesture. 'Rod, I love you. I'll do anything I have to do to get you to love me back. I don't care about all the other women you've known. I wouldn't even care about Pauline if you'd just say you care a bit about me.'

His lips twisted. 'I wish to hell I didn't,' he said. 'If I'd any sense I'd have stayed away altogether and settled for the kind of affair I'm used to handling. You're enough to

send any man round the bend, Claire. You don't play to
any accepted rules.'

'I'm not playing, that's why.' She slid her arms about his
neck again, putting her lips to his with desperate pleading.
'I've meant every word I've ever said to you. Why won't
you believe me?'

'Because I don't think you know the meaning of the
word.'

'And you do?'

'I'm not sure about that either. One thing I am sure of—
taking you to bed isn't going to make the issue any clearer.'

'You're afraid I'd use it as a lever to get you to marry
me?'

He shook his head. 'It isn't marriage I'm afraid of. If
I'm going to do it at all it ought to be now.' He took her
face between his hands, searching her features as if he
hoped to find the answer he was looking for right there.
'I've thought about it. I've thought about little else since
you left Mgala. Most men would call me a fool for hesitating in the circumstances.'

'But you're not most men,' she said softly. 'That's why
I love you so much. I'd be whatever you wanted in a wife.'

'Would you?' He smiled a little. 'Even if I proved to
have old-fashioned ideas about certain aspects?'

'If you mean you'd expect to wear the trousers, you
always have, haven't you?' Her own smile was reminiscent.
'You impressed that fact on me the first day we met.
Not that I didn't ask for it, I suppose. I really was the
spoiled brat you kept calling me. Remember when I threw
the coffee mug at you at Mgala? I think that was the first
time I began to realise I didn't even like myself very
much. I finally grew up that week, and you were the one
who made me.'

'Almost made you,' he corrected on a semi-humorous
note. 'Who have you been practising on since that night?'

'Nobody.' She was indignant. 'You don't imagine——'
The glint of laughter in his eyes stopped her. 'Swine!' she
said. 'You did that deliberately.' Her tone changed again,
the huskiness not assumed. 'I could satisfy you, Rod, I
know I could. Let me prove it.'

'You don't have to prove it. You had me almost over
the top just now.'

'But I *want* you to make love to me. Surely if we're
going to be married——'

'Are we going to be married?' The smile was still there,
but the note in his voice suggested an underlying serious-
ness. 'Are you so sure that's what you want?'

'Positive!'

Something in him seemed to relax suddenly. 'All right,
so we get married. No long engagements—I couldn't take
the strain. I'm due to go north in three weeks. It has to
be before then.'

'Any time you like.' She was filled with a bubbling
elation. Rod Gilvray's wife. It sounded wonderful!

She responded with abandonment when he kissed her,
feeling the immediate acknowledgment in him. His hands
were tender as they found their way inside the layers of
filmy material, moving over her skin with a touch which
set her whole body quivering. Then abruptly they were
gone, and he was lifting her to her feet and turning her
towards the door.

'I'm not making love to you now,' he said flatly. 'Not
before we get things straightened out.'

Claire twisted in his arms, hardly able to believe he was
sending her away. 'They are straightened out,' she pro-
tested. 'It's all been said.' She pressed herself urgently
against him, leaning her cheek against his bare chest to
hear the thudding of his heartbeats. 'Rod, you can't make
me go now. You can't!'

'I can,' he said. 'Just. I want to be able to look Bill in

the eye tomorrow without feeling a complete heel. I brought somebody with me, remember. We can't just ignore that fact.'

The rejection hurt even though she could see the reason for it. 'When are you going to tell her?' she asked.

'When I find the right moment.'

'You're not travelling back to town with her.'

His eyes narrowed a fraction. 'Are you asking me or telling me?' He didn't bother waiting for an answer. 'I'll deal with Pauline in my own way and my own time. Right?'

'Not if it means I can't tell Bill right away in the morning.' Claire kept her tone level, but the determination came through. 'You shouldn't have brought her in the first place.'

'I know darned well I shouldn't have brought her,' he agreed ruefully. 'It was a lousy way to use anybody. I had the crazy idea she might provide a nice safe barrier if necessary.'

'You mean if you'd found you didn't want me after all?'

'Something like that. Separation can play havoc with reality. I should have known how you'd react to any hint of competition. It's like showing a red rag to a bull.'

The fight went out of her suddenly. She said low-toned, 'If you want to change your mind you're free to do it.'

'I shan't change my mind.' There was a reassuring certainty in the statement. 'You might.'

'No!' She clung to him in fervent denial. 'There's no way I'll do that. I want to marry you more than anything else in the world!'

'That's all right, then,' he said softly. 'So just do as you're told and go on back to your own room, will you? Tomorrow might be a little difficult, but it won't last for ever. On Monday I'll tell Bill myself.'

It was going to be useless appealing to him any further:

Claire had to recognise that. She also had to acknowledge the fairness in his reasoning, and respect it.

'Oh God,' she said achingly, 'I do love you!'

'So you keep telling me.' His tone was dry. '*Will* you get out of here?'

'Only if you kiss me again first.'

'Claire'—there was exasperation in the sound—'if you don't——'

'So *I'll* kiss *you*.'

He put swift hands on her waist as she stepped towards him, holding her away to drop a fleeting kiss on her lips. 'That's all you're getting,' he said. 'I'm having enough trouble sticking to the straight and narrow as it is. Don't lose the enthusiasm, though. It's going to mean a lot.' He sighed when she made no attempt to relinquish her hold on his shoulders. 'Do I have to get tough?'

She laughed then, and shook her head. 'I'll go. But I hope it's going to be the last time you ever kick me out of your bed.'

'You can count on it.' His smile made her ache. He drew the back of his knuckles gently across her cheek and turned her once more to the door. 'Out!'

Claire went with reluctance. The house was still silent. She had no idea of the time. Hours could have passed, or mere minutes. Whatever, it made no difference to the outcome. She was going to marry Rod; the knowledge was like a light inside her.

The light was still there when she woke at eight to bright sunlight and the sound of birdsong outside her open window. Recollection of the conditions Rod had imposed brought a slight dampening, but it was something she had to accept. For today she must hug the knowledge to herself, supplemented only by the occasional shared glance with the man she loved. Frustrating when she wanted to shout it from the rooftops.

The sight of Pauline seated at his side at the breakfast table did nothing to help; the two of them were too much at ease with one another. It was only Rod's smile when he pushed across the butter she had requested that reassured her that last night had not been a dream. There would come a morning in the not very distant future when they would share a breakfast table for two and look at one another with shared memories of an even more intimate nature.

That thought kept her going through a frustrating morning. She wanted desperately to tell her father how things had worked out, yet knew that if she did so he was going to find it difficult to restrain himself from saying something to Rod about it. The more she dwelled upon it, the more unfair the restriction appeared to become. He was putting Pauline's feelings before hers. Why should she have to wait until he thought the time was ripe to impart the news?

Pauline herself seemed almost to underline that prior claim. Her attitude towards Rod was proprietorial to a degree which excluded any opportunity to get him alone. By lunchtime Claire was in a state bordering on anger. Rod had said earlier that he would be leaving around five to drive back to town. Having come with him, Pauline would naturally accompany him in the return journey. The thought of the two of them sharing the intimacy of his car all the way to Pauline's home was more than she could bear. Would Rod tell her on the way, or would he deem it kinder to do so over a quiet dinner somewhere this evening? And what form would their final farewell take?

It was during the afternoon when her control finally cracked. The men were practising putting on the nine-hole green Bill had recently had laid at the back of the house, while the women in the party chatted idly together over drinks on the terrace. Pauline was the one who brought matters to a head in choosing this particular opportunity to sort out what she obviously considered Claire's lack of comprehension regarding her own relationship with Rod.

'Of course we've known one another for quite some time,' she added casually after commenting on the demands made by the latter's job, 'but I've seen very little of him this year so far. We're going to have to make up for it now that he's back in England for a spell.'

'He's going to be up north,' Claire pointed out, holding on to her tongue at that point. 'What about your job?'

'Oh, I'm able to more or less work out my own schedule. That's no problem. I can organise my work to give me a few days here and there.' Pauline paused then, apparently feeling that as her point had been made she could afford something of a gesture. 'I'm organising a fashion show for the beginning of August. Tickets are limited, of course, but I could save you a couple. We'll be showing male fashions too. Perhaps you'd like to bring a friend along?'

The other women were engrossed in a discussion on bee-keeping, which Mary Lattimer had just taken up as a hobby. For Claire the sting in the tail of that last remark was just too much.

'August?' she repeated in bright enquiry. 'Oh, I'm afraid not, thanks. It would be rather a long way to travel for a single event. Anyway, as I'm sure you already know, Rod doesn't dress to suit any fashion but his own.'

The full impact didn't strike right away. Pale blue eyes took on a look of displeasure. 'You mean, you and your father are going with this job too?'

'Hardly. Bill didn't find himself an engineer of Rod's class in order to follow him around. I daresay he'll visit us from time to time—the way you intend to.' Claire laughed. 'We'll have to make sure we find a house or flat big enough to take visitors.'

In the blank moment following, Mary's voice came

across loud and clear: 'Oh, but it's worth all the hassel for the end product, believe me! You've never tasted anything as good. I'll let you have some and you can compare it with the named brands. I'm sure you'll agree with me.'

Pauline used a low tone when she did speak, her expression set and cold. 'What are you trying to tell me?'

'I'm not *trying* to tell you anything.' It was too late for regrets now; the damage was done. Claire could only put a brave face on it. She made herself look directly at the other. 'Rod asked me to marry him last night. I said yes.'

'Last night? But he didn't——' Pauline broke off, colour faintly tinging her skin as the implication sank in. 'I don't believe it!' she said flatly.

'Ask him.' Claire wasn't enjoying the triumph; it left a nasty taste in her throat. At the same time she doubted if Pauline would appreciate sympathy. She had a moment of trepidation when she thought about the way Rod was going to react, but it was too late to worry about that either. She had burned her boats with a vengeance.

Rod was coming back towards the terrace right now, Bill at his side, the two of them deep in conversation. Pauline watched them for a brief, tight-lipped moment before rising abruptly to her feet and moving to the french windows behind them.

'What's wrong with her?' asked Mary in surprise, having caught a glimpse of the younger woman's expression in passing. The surprise gave way to a knowing little smile when Claire failed to answer. 'Have you been saying something you shouldn't?'

'Has who been saying something they shouldn't?' asked Bill, coming up the steps. His glance went from the older to the younger face, brows lifting. 'Do I sense a certain atmosphere?'

Rod was looking at Claire too, his face expressionless. 'Where did Pauline go?' he asked.

'Indoors.' She couldn't bring herself to meet his eyes.

He asked no further questions. Leaving the putter he had been carrying up against the wall, he carried on into the house himself, a certain purpose in the set of his shoulders.

'What's been going on?' asked Bill quietly with his eyes still on his daughter. 'It's obvious something has.'

Claire put down her glass and got to her feet, her movements stilted. The smile she turned in the direction of the rest of the party felt pasted on. 'Will you excuse us for a few minutes?'

Bill followed her indoors and out into the hall. There was no sign of either Pauline or Rod. She chose the study because there was little chance they would have gone in there, leaning against the big desk to face her father with her lower lip caught between her teeth.

'You're going to find out soon enough, so I may as well tell you now,' she said. 'Rod and I are going to be married.'

He looked a little uncertain. 'So you said.'

'No, I mean it. It's arranged—or will be just as soon as we can get round to it.'

'Well, congratulations!' He still looked as if he weren't sure quite what was expected of him. 'If it's what you wanted, why the tragedy face? Have you changed your mind already?'

She pulled a wry face, shaking her head. 'We agreed to keep it quiet until after today for obvious reasons, but I'm afraid I just let the cat out of the bag to Pauline.'

Comprehension was swift, the censure tempered by a certain sympathy. 'Discretion was never your strong point, was it, darling? I gather she didn't take it very well.'

'No.' There was guilt in the statement. 'I just couldn't take the way she was talking about him—about *them*. Why should I have to? Rod had no right to expect it.'

'He had no right to bring her at all if he intended asking you to marry him,' came the abrupt comment. 'It isn't the kind of thing I'd expect from a man of——' He broke off, assessing her change of expression. 'Did he intend it?' he asked after a moment. 'Or was the decision forced on him?'

Claire flushed hotly. 'There was no pressure involved. He wants to marry me. He said he'd been thinking about it since the day I left Mgala.'

'But with enough doubt to bring another woman along with him in case he turned out to be wrong?' Bill paused consideringly, then shrugged. 'Well, I can see his point. You were thrown together under a certain duress in Africa. Things can look very different under more civilised conditions. Considering the circumstances, I'd say he was right in asking you to leave things in abeyance until he got Pauline off his hands.'

'Trust another man to see it that way!'

Her father smiled at her sadly. 'You're trying to hide from it, Claire. You're the one in the wrong, and you know it. It wouldn't have hurt you to let her finish out the weekend with her pride intact.'

'She had to know some time.'

'Now you're on the defensive. Of course she had to know some time, but in private where you wouldn't be likely to see her reactions. She might not have expected to marry him herself, but she was entitled to some consideration. If you agreed with Rod on that point last night you——'

The opening of the door cut off whatever else he was about to say. Rod paused on the threshold, face set in lines Claire recognised only too well. His glance went from her to her father and back again, losing nothing of its anger in the process.

'I want to speak to you, Claire,' he clipped. 'Alone, if you don't mind.'

'It's all right, I've already told Bill all about it.' Her tone was subdued. 'I'm sorry, Rod. I didn't mean it to happen.'

'No? According to Pauline, you took quite a delight in telling her in front of the others.'

'That's not true! They weren't even listening. I tell you it wasn't intentional.' She caught herself up, hearing the tremor in her voice with a swift sense of rejection. 'I'm not going to spend too much time doing penance over·it either. I've said I'm sorry.'

'And that covers it?' The look he gave her was searing. 'You always were more concerned with your own interests; God knows why I thought you'd be any different in this instance.' He stopped, visibly relaxing the hard set of his shoulders, eyes rueful as he remembered the other occupant of the room. 'Sorry, Bill. There's no reason why you should have to be involved in this.'

'She's my daughter,' came the mild reply. 'I suppose I might as well know the worst.' He moved towards the door. 'I'm going to let you two sort it out on your own.' Passing the other man, he paused, brows lifting quizzically. 'Is it still in order to say I couldn't be more pleased?'

The smile was returned, albeit briefly. 'Thanks.'

Claire waited until the door had closed behind her father before saying anything else, aware of a lightening of her heart. Of course Rod wouldn't change his mind over a little thing like this—any more than she would. She met his eyes with unconcealed appeal.

'I really didn't do it deliberately, Rod. I got caught on the raw, that's all. Believe me—please?'

'I believe you.' The anger had died although the compression was still there about his mouth. 'You've absolutely no sense of discretion, but I doubt if you're that vindictive.'

'I'm not. I'm really not.' She went to him swiftly, putting her arms about his neck and going on tiptoe to kiss him.

'Poor Bill! I think he thought my last hour had come! You looked so furious.'

'I was.' He held her for a moment, hands somewhat lacking in last night's tenderness, then put her away from him firmly. 'I still am. Intentionally or not, you put me in a lousy position. What kind of journey do you think we're going to have back to town now?'

'Strained.' There was a small part of her that couldn't help but feel glad about that. 'Couldn't she travel with the Lattimers when they go?'

'Why involve them?'

'I suppose you're right.'

'There's no suppose about it. I'm stuck with the situation. I ought to wring your neck!'

Claire was silent for a moment, sensing a certain lack of tolerance behind the seemingly philosophical acceptance. 'You know,' she said, trying to make light of it, 'you can be something of a bully at times. It's a good thing I love you enough to put up with it.'

Involuntarily his expression relaxed, his lips pulling into a reluctant smile. 'What am I going to do with you, Claire?'

'Love me,' she whispered. 'Just love me.'

'I do, dammit.' His voice was suddenly rough. He took hold of her and pulled her up to him, kissing her hard and demandingly on the lips. 'You're an infuriating little wretch, and there's every chance I'm going to have nothing but trouble with you, but you've got me hogtied. I think the sooner I get that ring on your finger the better. You don't mind a quiet wedding, do you? I'm not cut out for all the topper and tails stuff.'

'Whatever you like,' she said happily. 'I don't mind. Are we going to have a honeymoon before the job starts?'

'Yes, we are. Even if it's only a week on our own somewhere.' Rod had his face against her hair, his hands curving her hips, firm and possessive. 'I'll make the arrangements. How about a week tomorrow?'

Claire was beyond thinking straight, beyond thinking of anything but the emotions he could rouse in her with just a touch. 'Yes,' she said. 'Oh yes!' She ran her hands down his arms, loving the muscularity under her fingertips, slid them around his back and under his cotton shirt to reach the firm flesh beneath. The world became a blur as he found her lips again, sensation flooding through her. She wanted everything, and to give him everything. When he held her away from him this time she was almost ready to weep from sheer frustration.

'Not now,' he said softly, sounding considerably regretful himself. 'And not here.'

'Oh God!' There was a sob in her voice, partly of anger. 'You're always doing this to me!'

'I know.' The apology had a certain element of gratification mingled with it. 'We just don't seem able to get the timing right. I can't make love to you in your father's study with somebody likely to walk in any minute, much as I want to. It cuts both ways, sweetheart. I feel just as deprived.'

'Then don't go back to London,' she said. 'Stay tonight, Rod. Please!'

'I can't.'

'Because you have to take Pauline home?'

'No,' with a sigh. 'Because I have a job to do in the morning.'

'You can travel up with Bill in the car—let Pauline take yours. It's hired anyway, isn't it?'

'Yes, if that has anything at all to do with it.' He shook his head. 'No go. If I spend the night here I'm no more going to be able to stay away from you than fly.'

'I wouldn't want you to. Why do you think I'm asking?'

'What about Bill?'

'What about——' Claire caught herself up, biting her lip. 'It's only a week.'

'That's not the point. He wouldn't appreciate being taken for granted in his own home. We're going to have to wait.'

'But . . .' Claire began, and saw his jaw firm.

'I said no. You've got to realise you can't expect to get your own way every time we have a difference of opinion. Not that I wouldn't give quite a lot to indulge you in this particular instance,' he added with a wry expression.

She gave in because there was no alternative, aware of a faint area of doubt stirring at the back of her mind. Not a man you can wind around your little finger, Bill had said. Well, she wouldn't want him to be, but up to this moment she hadn't fully realised just how strong-willed he really was. She loved him, but there was no way she was going to become an extension of him in that sense. Marriage was a partnership, not a take-over. If she had to back down sometimes, then so did he. That was something they were going to have to sort out from the start.

'All right,' she said resignedly, 'I suppose you're right. I'm going to see you before next Monday, though, surely?'

'I hope so. Can you come up to town for an evening— maybe stay over?' He saw the look in her eyes and laughed, shaking his head. 'The hotel I'm staying in isn't the kind where they turn a blind eye to unregistered guests, and I happen to know they're fully booked through the rest of the month. Will you resign yourself to the inevitable? You'll be having what every bride is supposed to want— a wedding night to remember.'

'I'd remember it anyway,' she said, and rubbed her cheek pleasurably against his chin. 'Do husbands shave before they go to bed?'

'This one will.' He sounded amused. 'I'm a twice a day man in any case, as you've just found out. I could always grow a beard, of course. It shouldn't take long. Do you fancy being kissed through a faceful of hair?'

'Not by you—I like your aftershave. Anyway, you have enough hair on your head—to say nothing of this mat you wear on your chest!'

He caught her hand before she could unfasten more than one button. 'Behave yourself, will you.'

'I don't want to behave myself,' she said. Her eyes met his and melted. 'Rod ...'

The knock on the door sounded tentative. Rod lifted an ironical eyebrow at her before calling the invitation. Bill's head came round the door wearing an apologetic expression.

'Hope I'm not barging in too soon, but I thought you ought to know Pauline just took off for the station in a taxi she ordered up on the phone.'

'Lord, have we been in here that long?' Rod sounded disbelieving. He paused, obviously considering the pros and cons. 'Did she leave any message?'

'Yes.' The other man's smile was faintly embarrassed. 'But not one I'd like to repeat. I don't somehow think you'll be seeing Madame Barton again.'

'He wouldn't have anyway.' Claire slipped an arm through that of the man at her side, smiling brightly at her father. 'You can stop looking so pensive. I've been forgiven.'

The two men exchanged a glance of mutual understanding. 'Good luck,' Bill said with a grin. 'I've had twenty-two years of it.'

He hadn't, but somehow the old bitterness no longer registered. I love them both, Claire thought, and knew she had never been happier than at that moment.

CHAPTER SEVEN

THE honeymoon lasted ten days. Corfu had been Rod's choice because he had once spent a holiday there as a youth and retained fond memories of it; Claire had gone along with it because she had no particular preference for anywhere else. They stayed in a privately rented cottage in a small fishing village on the east coast, eating at the local tavernas or driving the hired car to a restaurant in one of the larger resorts, bathing from the rocky cove with its crescent of brown sand, getting to know one another in senses other than just physical.

For Claire, the latter was all she had dreamed about. In Rod's arms she discovered whole new elements of love and loving, delighting in her growing ability to please him in turn. The first time he had been gentle with her, rousing her with tenderness and control to a point where the fleeting agony of his first possession was almost a necessity. She had loved him the more for that forebearance, knowing how different it could have been had he considered only his own needs. In physical togetherness they were totally compatible.

Learning to live together proved a rather different matter. So many times during those first days did they manage to find points of contention. One of the things Claire discovered quite early on was Rod's possessiveness, when he caught her being chatted up by a couple of the Corfiot youths from the village.

'You didn't have to let them paw you,' he said in disgust after seeing them off the beach. 'You were enjoying it!'

'They didn't paw me,' Claire came back with alacrity.

114

'One of them put a hand on my arm, that's all. He was simply trying to emphasise what he was saying because I was being slow in translating.' She attempted to lighten the moment. 'Not surprisingly really, considering I only know a couple of dozen words of Greek! Talk about me Jane, you Tarzan!'

'It isn't funny,' he said. 'The women here don't encourage that kind of familiarity from men outside their own family. It's likely to be taken the wrong way.'

'So what am I supposed to do—ignore them altogether?'

'Unless I'm with you, yes. Not that they're likely to come across when we're together.'

'Especially if you start wearing your black belt,' Claire agreed with studied sarcasm. 'It's supposed to be universally recognised, isn't it?'

Rod shook his head, refusing to rise to the taunt. 'I'm not going to argue with you. If you can't see the common sense in what I've said I'll just have to make sure you don't go anywhere on your own, that's all.'

He did exactly that for the rest of their stay, and Claire had to accept it, fume against the restrictions it imposed on her movements though she might. Yet she had to admit that deep down a small part of her warmed to his assertiveness too. It made her feel protected, cherished, worried about in a way her father had never done.

They spent only three days in London on their return before travelling up north. With gloomy visions of likely winter conditions, Claire bought plenty of sweaters and pants in pure wool from Jaegar, teaming them with a hip-length sheepskin jacket and lined, knee-length boots.

'It's only August,' Rod pointed out in amusement when she showed her purchases to him the same evening. 'You could have bought all those in Leeds if you needed them.'

'I might need them sooner than you think,' she said. 'Colwood is pretty high up, isn't it?'

'The town itself isn't too bad. It's served by one of the main Leeds routes. Anyway, the house we're leasing does have central heating, believe it or not. It's quite civilised up there.'

She wrinkled her nose at him. 'Stop teasing me! I can't help having a preference for my own part of the world. I'm a hot-blooded southerner through and through!'

Looking at her standing there in the bedroom wearing nothing but flimsy bra and briefs in addition to the boots she had just been trying on, he smiled a slow smile. 'Right now, you're an incredibly fetching one.'

'Bill will be here in less than half an hour,' she warned as he moved towards her. Laughing, she backed away. 'Rod, we don't have time!'

'There's always time,' he said, and swung her up in strong arms to find her mouth in a kiss which brooked no denials. 'I want my wife and I'm going to have her—come what may.'

Going down to the hotel foyer some thirty-five minutes later, Claire wondered if it were true that a woman who had just been made love to revealed it to the world in her eyes for some time afterwards. Certainly there was a special glow in hers; she could feel it there. Glancing up at the man at her side in the lift, she was conscious of a thrill of pride in the fact that this tall, dark, oh, so masculine male belonged to her. She wanted to lift the hand lightly holding hers to her lips and kiss the long, lean fingers, remembering the feel of them on her body, the achingly swift arousal they could conjure up. The physical part of marriage might not be all that mattered, but it had to be vital. She couldn't imagine ever tiring of Rod's lovemaking.

Her father was waiting for them in the hotel lounge. He got to his feet as they approached, his glance sliding

from her face to that of his son-in-law and back again
with a certain satisfaction.

'Sun-bronzed and fit,' he commented. 'That should see
you through a northern winter.'

It was a good evening enjoyed by all. Listening to the
two men in her life talk over dinner, Claire was glad they
got along so well. She laughed when Bill suggested smil-
ingly at one point that they didn't leave it too long before
making him a grandfather, catching her husband's whim-
sical glance. A year at least on their own had been the
original decision, but she had the sudden feeling that
neither of them might want to wait as long when it came
to the point. The thought of having Rod's baby stirred
her immeasurably.

Later, brushing her hair at the dressing table mirror
prior to going to bed, she said tentatively, 'Bill's right, you
know, Rod. This eighteen months while we're in one place
would be the ideal time to start a family.'

'Bored with me already?' he asked on a light note which
drew an answering smile to her lips.

'You know that's not true.'

He came up behind her, putting his hands on her bare
shoulders to drop a kiss on the top of her head. 'I know,'
he said. He met her eyes through the glass and a flame
kindled, his fingers sliding down the tiny straps which sup-
ported her nightdress and curving to cup her breasts as the
material fell away from her, voice roughening. 'No babies,'
he said. 'Not yet. I want you to myself for a while.'

The familiar excitement was growing in her, firming
the flesh beneath his hands as she arched to his touch.
The nightdress slid down to her ankles when he drew her
to her feet, leaving her slenderly curving image reflected
in the mirror, smooth and golden in the soft light. Rod
was head and shoulders above her, his chest a broad hard

pillow on which she could lean while his hands moulded her possessively. This was all she wanted too right now. Just Rod, no one else. No one at all.

Colwood proved to be a thriving little market town set amidst some of the most glorious scenery Claire had ever seen. Instead of the draughty rural dwelling she had visualised, the 'cottage' Bill had arranged for them to rent turned out to be a modernised dream of a place with central heating and well equipped fitted kitchen. There were two spare bedrooms in addition to their own large double—plenty of room, as Rod said, to put up any visitors who happened to come their way. Most of the furniture was in oak, with a warming addition of chintz in the roomy sitting room with its wide stone fireplace and inglenooks. Claire wondered what kind of people could bear to leave the products of such obvious loving attention to the doubtful care of total strangers, and why.

The actual dam site was almost ten miles away, involving the flooding of a narrow valley which fortunately was unpopulated beyond one small farm already vacated. Work on the campsite was almost completed ready for the first of the teams moving in. Rod counted on three months of reasonable weather in which to complete the first stage of the dam construction itself, spending the worst of the winter on the diversion tunnel and leaving the greater part of the following year clear for the main part of the job.

Before the first week was out, Claire was already beginning to resent the demands made by the job on Rod's time, aware as she was of the necessity for his supervision. The townspeople themselves were slow to accept newcomers to their midst, although polite and courteous enough on the surface. Bumping into Dinah Shaw in the High Street self-service store that second Monday morning came as blessed relief. Older than Claire by seven or eight years, and possessed of a bright confidence, the other woman offered an immediate and welcome friendship with her invitation to coffee the following morning.

Over the next couple of weeks that friendship grew, extending to a small group of other women similarly grass-widowed. Dinah was married to a market trader who spent a great deal of the week travelling from one stall site to another during the summer months, with only Sundays to call his own. Their home was on the edge of town, newly built and luxurious with a superb view out over the Dale from the huge lounge window.

'I used to do the rounds with Reg when he first started out in the trade,' she confided to Claire on one occasion, 'but it got too much. He's up at five most mornings and doesn't get back till late. Worth it, I suppose, considering it got us all this'—waving an airy hand to encompass the expensively furnished room—'but I sometimes think moving so far out was a mistake in itself. At least there was plenty of entertainment in Leeds. You wait till you've had a winter here. We were snowed up for three days last one.'

'I'm not looking forward to it,' Claire admitted wryly. 'Not with Rod so busy.'

'Work comes first, love,' the other woman agreed, re-filling both coffee cups from the percolator. She looked up, pushing back the fall of short blonde hair from her face with a lift of her eyebrows. 'How about a spot of something to liven this stuff up? There's a new bottle of Tia Maria in the cocktail cabinet.'

About to refuse, Claire hesitated, unwilling to sound a wet-blanket. 'Just a dash,' she agreed after a moment, and laughed. 'I have to drive home.'

'You're not likely to get breathalysed in broad daylight round here,' Dinah said, crossing the room to open the mirror-lined cabinet and extract the correct bottle from among a vast collection. 'Anyway, you'd have to drink a tumblerful of this before it started reckoning. Do you want it separate or in the cup?'

'In the cup, please,' Claire requested, and stifled a protest as Dinah untipped the bottle in a far too generous measure. Too late now, short of throwing the whole lot away. But she needn't drink it all.

Tasting it, however, she had to admit that the liqueur did something for Dinah's somewhat indifferent coffee. She took another sip, longer this time, feeling the warmth slide down into her stomach and set up a relaxing little glow.

'Nice,' she said, and laughed suddenly. 'My father would have a fit if he saw me doing this! He thinks any kind of morning drinking is degenerate!'

Dinah shrugged. 'I never could see what difference the time of day makes myself. How about your husband? Does he have the same kind of ideas?'

'It never came up.'

'Well, I wouldn't bother asking him. Here, have a drop more.'

Too late to stop her, Claire said lightly, 'There must be more of that than coffee in here now.'

'The way I make coffee, Reg would call that a blessing in disguise,' came the unconcerned response. 'I don't know what it is I do wrong, but it never tastes the same as anybody else's. Are you going to be able to get to Mary Cawthorne's tomorrow?'

Claire waved an acknowledging hand. 'There's absolutely nothing to stop me.'

'Oh, good. No point in taking two cars when I have to practically pass your door to get there myself. I'll pick you up around ten-fifteen.'

'In that case you must come back with me to lunch,' Claire invited on impulse. 'Be nice to have company for a change.'

'Suits me.' Dinah sounded gratified. 'You know, we'll

all have to get together some time—the four of us, I mean. You and Rod, me and Reg.' The grin widened her full mouth. 'Maybe Ted and Alice too if they're lucky!'

'More new people?' queried Claire quite seriously, and received a speculative glance.

'Guess you never saw that film. Just a joke, love—take too long to explain. How about staying here for lunch today seeing I'll be coming to you tomorrow? It'll have to be pizza—I don't have much else in the freezer right now—but we could open a bottle of wine to go with it. You're not expecting Rod home to lunch, are you?'

Claire shook her head. 'He stays on site and eats with the men.'

'Believes in good labour relations, does he?'

'I don't think it's so much to do with that, just more convenient, that's all.' Claire lightened her tone. 'I'd love to stay, Dinah. Thanks.'

It was gone three when she eventually left for home, waving a laughing and slightly unsteady goodbye to Dinah through the car window as she pulled away, and thanking heaven for the automatic transmission. She had been tipsy before, but never in the middle of the day like this. She felt on top of the world.

The elation lasted until she was in the house, giving way abruptly to nausea as she closed the outer door behind her. She made it to the bathroom just in time, afterwards leaning her damp forehead against the coolness of the tiles and vowing never to mix that particular combination again. Rod wouldn't be home for another couple of hours at least, thank heaven. Perhaps if she just lay on the bed for a while this awful feeling would pass.

It was Rod's hurried entry into the bedroom which awoke her. She came up on an elbow with a start, wincing as pain shot through her head. The soft dull glow of evening filled the room.

'What's wrong?' he asked, coming to sit on the edge of the bed with a look of concern on his face. 'Are you ill?'

'I was sick,' Claire admitted with reluctance, and saw his expression change.

'You don't think . . .'

'No, I'm not pregnant,' she denied, and thought he looked almost disappointed for a moment. 'I just don't feel too good, that's all.'

He studied her, expression altering yet again. 'Have you been drinking?'

'Only wine at lunch,' she defended.

'How much?'

'A glass.' She met his eyes and coloured a little. 'All right then, two or three to be exact. We shared a bottle.'

He said dryly. 'That might explain the way the car's parked. Another couple of inches and you'd have been over the bank. Who's we?'

'Dinah Shaw. I went over for coffee and she asked me to stay to lunch.'

'Mostly liquid by the sound of it. You could have had a nasty accident driving home in that condition.'

'I wasn't drunk, just sick.'

'You were sick because you were drunk,' came the flat statement. 'And I'd be willing to bet you had more than wine. Right?'

Claire nodded resignedly. 'I think it might have been the Tia Maria that made me ill. It didn't mix well with the pizza.'

'You don't say!' Rod's shudder was not wholly play-acting. 'Was your friend Mrs Shaw ill too, by any chance?'

'Not when I left. I shouldn't imagine so. I think she's probably more used to it than I am.'

'Is she indeed?' There was a sudden edge to his voice which had not been there before. 'I think it's perhaps time I met this new friend of yours.'

'Dinah suggested the four of us get together some evening. You'll like her. She's fun.' Claire pushed herself upright, wrinkling her brows as the throbbing in her head increased. 'I must get supper ready. You must be famished.'

'Stay there, I'll get it.' Quite gently he pressed her down into the pillows again. 'What were you planning on having?'

'Grilled pork chops and corn-on-the-cob. The salad is ready in the fridge—I did that this morning.' She watched him move across the room, added guiltily, 'I'm sorry, darling. Are you sure you can manage?'

'Probably better than you can,' he said from the doorway with a hint of mockery in his smile. 'Think you might manage a little yourself?'

'Not the pork, perhaps some salad.'

'And coffee?'

'It was Claire's turn to shudder. 'Make it tea. The very smell of coffee would turn me over!'

'Good,' he observed with sympathy. 'It might make you think twice before indulging in that stuff again. I'll bring yours up before I start on mine, then I can keep the doors closed and stop the cooking smells from filtering through the house. We still need a replacement blade for the extractor fan.'

'Oh lord, I meant to stop off in town on my way home from Dinah's and get one,' Claire exclaimed. 'I'll do it tomorrow.'

'No,' he said, 'I will. That way I'll be sure of having it.'

'Please yourself,' she flung after him resentfully as he left the room, and immediately felt ashamed. He had asked her on three separate occasions to fetch the new blade he had ordered from the local electrical supplies, and each time something had happened to put it out of her mind. She could hardly blame him for losing patience.

Ten minutes later he appeared again bearing a tray set

out neatly with a plate of salad, brown bread and butter and the tea things.

'Sure this is going to be enough for you?' he asked, letting down the short legs which converted the whole thing into a bed-table and placing it across her.

'More than enough,' Claire assured him, not feeling like eating at all. 'I'll get up when I've finished and do the clearing.'

Rod shook his head. 'Not necessary. The best thing you can do is get undressed and into bed properly. A good night's sleep will put you right.' His smile was without censure. 'Believe me, I know what I'm talking about.'

Claire put a hand over his, expression penitent. 'Thanks for not being angry.'

'I might be if it happened on a regular basis,' he replied lightly. 'I'd better get downstairs. I left the chops under the grill.'

She didn't see him to talk to again that evening because she was in bed and asleep before he came up to take the tray. Waking some time during the night, she felt the comforting wall of his back up against hers and lay for a long time thinking how much she loved this man before finally drifting off to sleep again.

By morning she was back to normal again and feeling sheepish about the whole affair. Rod made no comment, but did enquire what she was planning on doing that day. She told him reluctantly, half expecting an adjoinder to leave the wine alone this time, but he passed up on that opportunity also. No doubt he took it that once was more than enough for anybody but a complete idiot.

Dinah turned up at ten-fifteen looking entirely herself. Claire refrained from mentioning her own ill-effects because it seemed so ridiculous in retrospect. They hadn't, after all, drunk so much.

There were five of them altogether at the Cawthorne

place, and coffee and biscuits only on the menu. Mary Cawthorne's husband was a local builder who had, as Mary herself resignedly put it, started a dozen jobs in his own home and finished none. At the moment she had canvas sheets draped over the kitchen bay which he was in the middle of extending outwards. She apologised for the mess in the manner of one long accustomed to doing so and served coffee in a sitting room which had a red brick chimney breast half covered in stone facing. Different, as she cheerfully acknowledged.

Claire enjoyed the couple of hours or so they spent together, but had to admit to herself that once a week would be as much as she could take of this kind of thing. Having no children to talk about as yet, and being totally uninterested in the comparative performance of one brand of kitchen appliance against another, she felt distinctly out of it. Dinah, she was relieved to note, appeared to share the same reservations.

'They're okay,' she commented on the way back to Claire's temporary home, 'but in small doses only. God forbid I ever get to the point where I get excited over a new dishwasher!'

'Did you ever consider starting a family?' Claire asked casually, and received an emphatic shake of the head in reply.

'No way. I'm not cut out to be a mother.'

'How about Reg?'

'He wouldn't be having them. He'd hardly even see them. No, he got his way about moving out here from town, but I'm not getting myself saddled with a couple of kids just to please him.' Dinah glanced sideways at her passenger. 'How about you? Do you want children?'

'We both do,' Claire said softly. 'But not just yet.'

'Well, at your age you've plenty of time to think about it. Rod's quite a piece older, didn't you say?'

'Only ten years.'

'Same age as Reg. Good-looking?'

Claire laughed. 'It depends on your tastes. He isn't what people call handsome. I suppose you could say his features are too masculine for that.'

'Sounds just my type.'

Claire took the remark as a joke. It was the kind of thing Dinah was apt to say.

She had already prepared a fresh ham salad for lunch because the day was so warm. They ate out on the little patio at the rear of the house, seated at the wrought iron table which had come as part of the furnishings, with the best glasses sparkling in the sunshine. Claire had hesitated over opening the wine, but it seemed so mean not to do so considering Dinah's obvious liking for a drink with her meal, and she didn't need to take more than a sip or two herself.

'Kindred spirits,' said Dinah, watching her pour. 'I'm glad you came to Colwood, Claire.'

She was finishing off the last of the bottle when Rod walked round the corner of the house. Glass half raised to her lips, she ran an appraising, totally unabashed eye over him as he came towards them, a smile tilting her lips.

'You were right,' she said without bothering to lower her voice. 'He's all male!'

Conscious of the wine bottle still on the table and the accusing empty glass in front of her, Claire performed hasty introductions.

'You didn't say you'd be home to lunch,' she tagged on. 'There's nothing wrong out at the site, is there?'

Rod shook his head, sliding the small parcel he had been carrying on to the table and pulling out the spare chair. 'I came through to pick this up. They're usually closed by the time I get back to town at night.' His glance rested briefly on Claire's glass before lifting to her face without expression. 'Enjoying yourselves?'

Dinah waved her own glass. 'Sorry we didn't leave you any.'

'I'll make some coffee,' Claire said hastily. 'It won't take long.'

In the kitchen she quickly got things together, trying not to think about what Rod was going to say when he got her alone this evening. He might not even believe that she had only drunk half a glass of wine herself, although he should be able to see for himself that she was very far from yesterday's state. Anyway, he had no right to be here at this time of day, she thought defensively. Spying on her, that was all it was. Picking up the fan blade was just an excuse!

She could hear the murmur of Dinah's voice through the window, and the deeper tone answering her in what sounded like monosyllables. Did Rod have to be so un-friendly to her friend? After all, it was entirely because of his job that they were stuck here in the back of beyond at all. Surely he didn't begrudge her a little fun!

It was difficult to tell what he was thinking when she went outside again. Dinah was leaning back in her chair looking faintly put out, her glass empty in front of her.

'We've been getting acquainted,' she said. 'You never told me your father owned the contracting firm building the dam.'

'It never came up.' Claire put out the cups and saucers and began to pour the coffee, her hand nervous under Rod's gaze. 'Oh darn!' she exclaimed as some of his spilled over on to the saucer. 'I'll have to get a cloth.'

'Don't bother,' he said, and removed the cup to pick up the saucer and toss the dregs on to the grass a few feet away. There was a line to his mouth which Claire didn't like very much.

He made no attempt to move as time wore on, responding politely enough to Dinah's overtures but revealing little interest in furthering any particular topic of conversation. It was Dinah herself who finally broke up the party by saying she had another call to make before going home. She sounded piqued, apparently unaccustomed to having any man take as little notice of her as Rod was doing.

'He seems to have something on his mind,' she said to Claire at the car. 'It's my guess he has a bone to pick with you. I know the symptoms. If you'll take my advice, attack is the best means of defence where men are concerned. It disconcerts them.'

Right at that moment it seemed very good advice. Claire went back to the patio with righteous indignation growing inside her.

'All right,' she said the moment she rounded the corner, 'so you saw what you came home to see. I had exactly half a glass, but I don't suppose you're going to believe that for a moment!'

'Certainly I believe it,' Rod came back evenly, taking the wind right out of her sails. 'And cut out the belligerence. I called home because I happened to be close enough to take the opportunity, that's all. Incidentally, I haven't eaten yet.'

'That's your own fault,' Claire pointed out on a stiff note. 'I can hardly have a meal prepared when I don't even know you're going to be here. There isn't going to be time to do anything much if you have to get back.'

'I shan't bother going back,' he said. 'Not now. Anything that crops up Graham will have to deal with.' He studied her for a moment, brow lifting. 'An omelette will do.'

Resentment flooded her. 'You know where the kitchen is,' she retorted. 'This isn't a restaurant!'

He didn't follow her indoors straight away. When he

finally appeared in the sitting room doorway, Claire was pretending an absorbed interest in a magazine page, head bent so that she didn't see his face.

'You've got it upside down,' he said, coming across to take it from her and turn it the right way up. He sat down on the chair opposite, looking at her with a patiently controlled expression. 'Let's get something straight, shall we, Claire? I don't expect you to run this place like a hotel. Far from it. But if it's my job to go out and earn the wherewithal to buy food it's surely not too much to ask that you cook it.'

'You didn't ask,' she defended. 'You demanded!'

'If that's what it sounded like it certainly wasn't meant to.'

'Well, it did.'

Patience gave way suddenly to intolerance, his mouth narrowing. 'It didn't take long for the novelty to wear off, did it? I suppose what you'd really like is the same kind of set-up you had before we were married—somebody to fetch and carry for you all the way down the line!'

'So what if I would?' she demanded with heat. 'I'm obviously not going to get it.'

'No, you're not. You've got Mrs Jones coming in twice a week to do the bulk. What's left shouldn't overtax your capabilities—always providing you don't spend all your time drinking, that is. And while we're on that subject, I don't much care for your choice of friends.'

'Really?' Claire was sitting on the extreme edge of her seat, eyes blazing. 'Well, too bad! My choice of friends is *my* affair!'

'But who you bring into this house is mine,' he came back hardily. 'She's too old for you, for one thing.'

'So are you,' she flashed, wanting to hurt. 'You sound more like a father than Bill ever did!'

'Small wonder, the way you're acting.' His tone was

scathing. 'I really began to think you'd grown out of that spoiled brat stage but I see I was wrong. You still have the mentality of a teenager.'

'Then it's a pity you married me!'

'That's one point we agree on.' Rod got to his feet, face hard set. 'I'm going back to the site. Don't bother about supper. I'll eat out.'

Claire stayed where she was as he left the room, unable to say the words which would bring him back. There was a lump as big and hard as a tennis ball in her throat. He hadn't meant it, of course, any more than she had meant it. He couldn't have—could he?

Hearing the slam of the car door, she wanted to get up and rush out after him, but pride held her back. They had both said things to regret. Why should she be the one to apologise first? By the time Rod came home he would have cooled down and they could talk things out rationally. The threat to eat out had been an idle one, she was sure. He would be home at the usual time.

She took special pains with the evening meal, preparing his favourite steak and kidney pie despite the warmth, and thanking heaven that her pastry decided to turn out right for once. At six she laid the table in the bow-windowed dining room, using the glassware and crockery she had brought with her from home. Most of their wedding presents were in storage at Meadowbank and would stay there until the day they acquired a place of their own— if that day ever came. Following a man wherever his job took him sounded all very well in theory, but in practice it could prove a different matter. That was something else they were going to have to discuss some time.

By seven-thirty she knew he wasn't coming home. Not for supper, at any rate. In a fit of pure white-hot anger, she took the whole pie out to the dustbin and threw it in, closing the lid on the appetising smell rising from the broken crust with a bang which must have been heard halfway round the town.

With the table cleared and everything put away, there was no sign that a meal had ever been prepared. At nine Claire went upstairs and took a bath, then got into bed and just lay there waiting until she finally heard the car drive up around a quarter to ten.

Rod didn't come up right away. She heard him moving around below, the sound of doors opening and closing, and then after a few minutes more a drift of music. He was listening to the radio, she thought furiously. That was how much he cared. Well, damn him. She would show him how little *she* cared too.

She was lying on her side with her back towards the door when he did come up some time later. He undressed without bothering to turn on the light, shaved in the bathroom as he always did, and ran the shower for what seemed like an age. Claire steeled herself not to move when the mattress tilted to his weight, clutching the edge to stop herself from rolling down the slight incline towards him. She sensed that he was lying on his back, an arm only inches away from hers. The faint tang of his aftershave tantalised her nostrils.

'You're not asleep,' he said suddenly. 'Your breathing is too fast.' When she didn't answer, he rolled over on to his side, putting out a hand to pull her on to her back and holding her there firmly in spite of her resistance. It was impossible to assess his expression in the darkness, but his voice was lacking in anger. 'We're not going to sleep on it, Claire. It's no solution.'

'Neither is anything else,' she said, low-toned but vicious. 'I don't want you touching me!'

'That's unfortunate,' he said, 'because I want to touch you.'

'You can't have things all your own way!'

'Very true. None of us can.' The smile was slow. 'We'll work on that basis from now on.'

She stiffened when he kissed her, keeping her lips tightly closed against him. But he wasn't brooking any refusals, regardless of what he had just said. Her resistance lasted only a moment or two before melting suddenly into passion, hot and mounting.

'I hate you,' she murmured as he removed her night-dress, and heard his low laugh.

'I know. I hate you too. We'll have to learn to live with it.'

CHAPTER EIGHT

THEY lived with it for all of a week, the quarrel never mentioned yet not forgotten either—at least not on Claire's part. She saw Dinah a couple of times, but made no attempt to invite her back to the house, not quite certain enough of herself to ignore Rod's statement. There was every chance that he had allowed anger to override judgment in Dinah's case. After all, he had only met her the once. How could anyone decide another's total character on such a flimsy basis?

In the rush to get the foundations of the dam down before the winter set in, Rod was staying longer and longer hours out at the site, determined that nothing should go wrong for want of better forward planning. Claire made no complaint, but the resentment grew in her daily. She had seen more than this of him in Africa. Surely it couldn't be necessary for him to spend quite so much time at work? He was putting the job before her—before their whole marriage.

The fine weather broke towards the weekend, bringing two days of intermittent rain and cold winds. Dinah rang on Friday morning sounding anything but downhearted.

'Reg has promised to knock off early because of the weather,' she announced, 'and we've got friends coming out from Leeds to spend the weekend. Calls for a celebration, I'd say. It'll have to be tonight, though. They're forecasting a break for tomorrow, so my better half will be off at the crack of dawn to make up for lost revenue. Can you and Rod make it?'

133

'It depends on what time he gets home,' Claire said resignedly. 'It could be late.'

'No problem. Just drift along when you can.' There was a pause and a slight change of tone. 'You do want to come, don't you?'

'Heavens, yes!' Claire could say it with conviction on her own behalf. 'It's ages since I went to any sort of party.'

'Then we'll have to make sure you enjoy this one. I'm trying to get hold of my brother Tony. He's been threatening to come and spend a few days with us for some time. You and he would get along—he's a real livewire. Anybody else you can think of who might swell the numbers?'

'The Cawthornes?' Claire ventured, and heard a snort of derision over the wire.

'Not this time, sweetie. Mary's idea of a knees-up stops at two glasses of cooking sherry! Never mind, I think I've covered all those who're likely to contribute. Prestburys are delivering a buffet, so don't bother eating supper first. See you tonight.'

Claire put down the receiver and stood for a moment contemplating the instrument undecidedly. She could always make sure Rod would be home in time by phoning him now and telling him about the party, but he had asked her on more than one occasion not to do so unless in an emergency, and putting his back up by ignoring the request was hardly the best way to present the idea. Still, it shouldn't make all that much difference. With no meal to prepare she could be ready herself when he did come home, and it wouldn't take him long to change. She desperately wanted to go to this party. It sounded fun, and she was badly in need of that particular commodity. No matter how late they were she would still insist on going.

She heard the car just before eight as she put the finishing touches to her face in front of the dressing table mirror. The dress she had chosen to wear was knee-length and low-cut at the back, revealing the tan she had kept up on the rear patio this last few weeks. Her hair hung glossily to her shoulders, almost black against the white material. She had contemplated having it cut, but Rod liked long hair on a woman. One more sacrifice she had made just to please him.

She ran downstairs as he came through the door, and saw his eyes light appreciatively as he viewed her.

'Nice to come home to,' he said. 'What's the occasion?'

'We're going to a party.' She said it quickly, giving him no time to react. 'Dinah only decided this morning, so there was no chance to let you know without phoning through, and I hardly thought it constituted an emergency. You've plenty of time to change, we're eating there.'

The smile faded from his lips, his expression firming. When he spoke it was quietly enough but on a note which left no room for misinterpretation. 'I don't think so, thanks. I'm tired and I'm hungry, and that's no mood to go party-ing in.'

'*You're* tired!' Claire was quivering with anger, know-ing he meant it. 'So am I! Tired of being married to a stick-in-the-mud engineer who'd rather spend his time poring over blueprints than anything else!'

'Not *anything* else,' he came back sardonically. 'You should know that.'

Her eyes were sparkling, her face flushed and tense. 'All I know is you make me sick!' she flung at him viciously. 'If you won't come I'll go on my own!'

He made no move to stop her as she caught up the light coat and handbag she had placed ready on the hall table and stalked past him. The sight of his car parked across the front of her own gave her momentary pause, but not for long. She could get round it by driving across the front lawn and through the low shrubbery on to the road. Anything rather than acknowledge defeat.

She had been almost certain she had left her keys in the ignition earlier, but they weren't there when she got into the car. A search through her handbag proved fruitless as she had known it would, having put into it only a few items she required for the evening not half an hour earlier. They were probably in the kitchen, she decided. That was where she had gone right after coming from shopping this afternoon. It meant going back indoors to fetch them, but so what? Rod could please himself what he did. She was going to the party.

There was no sign of him when she let herself back into the house. The sitting room door was closed, so she assumed he was in there. Her search of the kitchen proved no more fruitful. The car keys simply weren't there. Claire paused at the sink after closing the last cupboard door, gazing out at the hills as she tried to think.

'These what you're looking for?' queried Rod from the doorway behind her.

He was dangling the missing keys by the ring from a forefinger when she turned, face expressionless. She stared at him seethingly, sensing the mockery even if it wasn't visible.

'You had them all the time!' she accused. 'You knew I couldn't take the car!'

'Not unless you were more conversant with what goes on under the bonnet than you appear to be,' he agreed mildly. 'You'll be leaving them in the ignition once too often. It's an open invitation to any passing fancier.'

'It's my car,' she defended, too incensed to admit to the justice of what he was saying. 'At least, I understood it was.'

'It's in your name, yes. That doesn't mean I have to stand

by and watch you give it away to the first comer.'

'Don't be ridiculous! If anyone wanted it badly enough they'd get into it with or without the keys!'

'I daresay. The idea is to make it as difficult as possible.' He moved impatiently. 'I'm not standing about arguing that point. If you can't see sense in it it's useless anyway. Seeing there doesn't seem much chance of getting any supper, I'll run round to the Chinese take-away. Do you want anything?'

'I'm going to Dinah's party,' Claire said between her teeth. 'If you won't give me those, I'll use the spare set.'

'You lost them over a week ago, remember?' Rod looked at the keys still dangling from his finger, then closed a firm hand over them and put them in his pocket. 'You're not going to any party on your own—and certainly not that woman's.'

'Why?' she demanded. 'What have you got against Dinah? You only met her once.'

'That was once too often.' He studied her for a moment, mouth grim. 'Let's just say I don't care for women who make passes at other women's husbands the moment their backs are turned.'

'Dinah did?' She was nonplussed for a few seconds, then she rallied. 'You must have taken her too seriously. She jokes a lot.'

'She wasn't joking.'

'Have it your own way.' Claire paused before adding with control. 'A wedding ring doesn't give you any right to dictate to me about anything, Rod. I like Dinah. She's the only friend I've got in this place.'

'All right, so go on seeing her. Just don't expect me to like her too, that's all.'

Head up, she held out a hand. 'So can I have my keys, please?'

'No,' he said flatly. 'I already told you, no party without

me. Not the kind this one is likely to turn out to be, at any rate.'

'You're pre-judging without evidence. Is that fair?'

'I don't give a damn whether it's fair or not. It's the way I see it.' He paused, a hand on the doorknob. 'Do you want anything bringing in?'

'No,' she said furiously. 'I don't want *any*thing from you! You can sleep in the spare room tonight!'

One dark brow lifted mockingly. 'No way. If you want to sleep on your own, *you* move into the spare room. There's even a lock on the door.'

'And I'll make sure I use it,' she flung after him.

She stood irresolute for several moments after he had left the house, going over the whole episode in her mind with steadily mounting rage. He wasn't going to stop her, she decided at length. If she couldn't use the car there were other ways of getting across town to Dinah's.

The taxi firm promised to have a car round in fifteen minutes at the outside. The take-away was a ten-minute drive each direction, but at this time of the evening there would more than likely be a queue. At least she had to hope so. She watched for the vehicle through the sitting room window, coat on ready for a quick dash the moment she saw it turn the corner. Rod didn't know Dinah's address, so he could hardly follow her, even if he guessed where she had gone. A faint shame stirred in her, swiftly smothered. So what if she was behaving atrociously? He had driven her to it. He simply didn't have the right to tell her where she could or could not go.

The taxi came round the corner just as the long case clock out in the hall began to chime the quarter, followed close behind by Rod in the car. Deflatedly, Claire watched him get out and approach the taxi, saw him bend to speak to the driver through the opened window and knew that the game, so to speak, was up. She didn't stay to see any more. There didn't seem much point. Going upstairs, she began moving essential items through into the largest of the two spare bedrooms, tossing clean linen from the closet on to the unmade bed.

If she had expected Rod to come storming upstairs to confront her when he did come in, she was to be disappointed. He went straight through to the kitchen instead and began clattering plates around. A delicious aroma floated up to Claire, making her suddenly conscious of her empty stomach. She hoped it choked him, she told herself fiercely.

With her bed made there was little else to do but sit on it and twiddle her thumbs. Just before ten she heard the telephone ring. That would be Dinah phoning to find out what had happened to them, she surmised. She didn't go to the door because Rod would have heard her open it. Whatever excuse he made, it was obviously a brief one, because the ding of the replaced receiver came almost immediately.

Imagining Dinah's reaction only served to increase Claire's righteous anger. No way would Dinah ever allow herself to be put in this position. If necessary she would have walked out of the house and caught a bus. Too late for that now anyway. Too late for any gesture beyond the one she was already making.

Lying awake listening to the firm tread of Rod's steps when he came up around eleven, Claire steeled herself for the moment when her door would open. Sleeping on it was no solution, Rod had said the other night. Well, all right, she could go along with that. But he needn't think he was going to settle this as easily as he had settled the other. They had to come to some definite understanding first.

The house had been silent for more than half an hour before she finally acknowledged that he wasn't going to come. He was leaving her to stew, going back to his own words. She turned on her side and tried to ignore the empty feeling inside her. If that was the way he wanted it, that was the way it would be. She could hold out just as long as he could.

That latter statement was one she was to review with bitter irony over the following few days. From the way Rod acted they might have been sleeping in separate rooms since they were first married. Certainly it didn't seem to bother him too much. The apparent indifference hurt more than any amount of invective could have done, yet pride wouldn't allow her to make any overtures towards him. If she was guilty then so was he.

His announcement halfway through the week of an overnight trip to London came unaccompanied by any invitation to join him, and Claire refused to ask.

'Give Bill my love,' she said stiffly on the morning of his departure. 'Tell him I might be paying him a visit before too long myself.'

There was no reaction to that threat either. Rod simply nodded briefly and picked up his overnight case. Whether he would have attempted to kiss her goodbye or not she had no idea, because she didn't give him the opportunity, going into the sitting room and closing the door between them. A moment or two later she heard the car start up, and sat listening to the diminishing sound of the engine with a dryness in her throat. She wouldn't be one whit surprised, she told herself, if he had already contacted Pauline to tell her he was going to be in town. Tonight he might find the kind of solace he needed. Well, let him. She wouldn't be stuck for entertainment either, although it would hardly be of the same kind.

Contacting her on Monday, Dinah had sounded cheerfully unaware of any strain about their relationship, merely saying what a shame it was that they had not been able to make the party as it had been a really good evening. Rod, it appeared, had said only that he had arrived home too late to make it worthwhile. If Dinah privately thought that a lame excuse she kept the thought to herself. She bore Rod no obvious ill-will.

Phoning her today, Wednesday, Claire felt just a little uncertain of how to approach the subject. In the end she stated the bald truth. She was on her own and in need of companionship. Were Dinah and Reg free to come over for supper?

'We are,' said Dinah, 'but I've a better idea. My brother Tony is spending the week. How about us picking you up and going on from there? He was looking forward to meeting you Friday night after all I'd told him about you. This will help compensate.'

Claire's hesitation was fleeting. Why not? Another man's attention was just what she needed to take her mind off Rod's lack of it. 'All right,' she said, 'I'd like that. What time?'

'Say around eight-thirty. There's a new pub out on the Richmond Road Reg wants to take a look at. American roadhouse style, they say. We can come back here for supper afterwards, then Tony will drive you home.' Her tone warmed. 'Though I say it myself, he's quite something, that brother of mine! You two will get on like a house on fire.'

Something vaguely troubled Claire as she put down the receiver. Nothing she could put her finger on, just a feeling. Not concern over what Rod might think, for certain, she told herself. He had left her to her own devices; he could scarcely blame her for making the best of a bad job.

The day passed slowly. Claire did some shopping and took a couple of Rod's suits to the dry-cleaners, feeling a glow of self-congratulation that she had not allowed pettiness to overrule her. The weather had turned warm enough again to merit a couple of hours spent sunning herself on the patio, but the book she took out with her could not hold her interest.

Fundamentally speaking, there had been little alteration in her life style, she realised, thinking about it. She was just as bored as she had ever been, and certainly no happier. Her own fault? she wondered. Had she perhaps expected too much from marriage? But then it wasn't marriage itself she found so disappointing, was it? It was the humdrum existence Rod expected her to lead while he indulged the first love of his life—his work. He was like her father in that respect. She should have seen it from the first. Bill had never changed. No doubt Rod wouldn't either, not now. It was too late. That acknowledgment held little comfort.

She was ready and waiting when the Shaws arrived. Tony was only a couple of years older than Claire herself, tall and lithely built with a crop of dark curly hair and Travolta-type good looks. The black curve of a moustache suited him.

From the look in the bold blue eyes when Dinah introduced them, he found her equally worthy of a second glance.

'For once you didn't exaggerate,' he commented to his sister.

Reg Shaw was a big, talkative man with thinning brown hair carefully brushed across the top and a rather loud style of dress.

'Nice,' he said, running an appraising glance over Claire's silky pants suit. His laugh jarred. 'Bet that didn't come off any market stall!'

'Shut up, Reg,' his wife told him sharply. 'Let's get off.'

The two men sat together in the front of the car on the outward journey, leaving the women to share the rear

seat. Leaning against the leopardskin covers, Claire tried
to conjure a lighthearted mood, failing miserably because
she knew she shouldn't be here. From the way Tony had
greeted her she had the feeling he might be reading more
into her need for company during her husband's absence
than she had intended. Not that she could blame him if
he did. It certainly looked that way, when she thought about
it.

Reg started telling a joke as he drove, long and compli-
cated and punctuated by chuckles as he kept remembering
the punchline. Claire failed to recognise the latter when
it did come, and was a second or two late in joining in
the laughter, but nobody seemed to notice. Told by Tony,
the next contribution proved to be funny if more than a
little coarse. In her eagerness to make up for any implied
lack of appreciation last time, Claire started laughing almost
before the final words were out of his mouth, only realising
what he was actually saying when it was too late. Even
Dinah was moved to murmur an indulgent word of re-
proval.

'Glad somebody's got a sense of humour,' came the unabashed retort, accompanied by a grin over his shoulder
at Claire. 'Good, eh?'

Unable to refute the impression she had given, Claire
smiled back weakly and hoped he wouldn't allow his
apparent success to go to his head. The last thing she
desired was to be on the receiving end of any more so-
called jokes like that one.

The new public house turned out to be mock everything
except prices. Even the stone walls looked reconstituted.
There were three separate bars, with a disco-type floor
for dancing in one of them and a huge jukebox blaring out
sound.

'Drinks first,' said Tony, 'then we'll have a go.' He
caught the eye of a blonde-haired girl already on the floor

and let his own eyes travel the length of her curvaceous body in the skintight pants and matching sleeveless sweater. 'Some nice local talent you've got,' he commented, not bothering to keep his voice down.

Claire drank her gin and tonic quickly when it came, needing the kind of relaxation only alcohol could bring. It didn't seem to have much effect, so she had another, this time feeling a definite easing up of tension before she was halfway down the glass. By the time Tony decided he wanted to dance, she was in a mood to accompany him on to the floor without protest, though not too far gone to avoid the arms which immediately attempted to enfold her. Dinah had already told her that her brother worked at a disco in Leeds and often gave demonstrations in the art of disco dancing. She used that knowledge now to take his mind off his present more intimate inclinations, smiling at him challengingly.

'This is just your kind of beat, by all accounts. How about showing me how good you are?'

He needed no twice asking, breaking into a routine which left Claire metaphorically standing. Within a couple of minutes he had attracted enough attention to clear the floor. Claire stood back too, knowing herself no match for his expertise.

The applause was enthusiastic when he called a halt, people crowding about him to congratulate him and comment on his likeness to the star everybody knew by name. Claire was self-conscious when they began dancing again, aware that he was toning down his movements to suit hers and feeling inadequate.

'You ought to go and ask that blonde girl for a dance,' she said when they were seated again with the others. 'She looks good too.'

'And not just at dancing,' put in Reg with a guffaw

which drew his wife's remonstrative frown. 'She fancies you, right enough, Tone. Hasn't taken her eyes off you for ten minutes!'

'They're ten a penny like her down at the Crazy Horse,' returned his brother-in-law dismissively. He winked at Claire. 'Give me a bit of class any day of the week!'

It was gone eleven by the time they got back to Dinah's for supper. Not having eaten earlier, Claire was famished, and made sizeable inroads into the savoury pie and salad Dinah had prepared before going out. There was wine to accompany the food as a matter of course, but she managed to get away with half a glass again, thankful when Dinah served coffee to finish.

Around midnight she made the first tentative suggestion that she ought to be going home, but nobody would hear of it. Dinah put on another record and urged her husband on to his feet, draping herself about his neck with a giggle. She seemed somehow different tonight, Claire thought, watching the two of them from the sofa. Without being able to tie down the difference, she had to reluctantly concede that she didn't like her as much.

Tony ran a hand slowly down her bare arm, eyes glinting in the dimmed lighting. 'You're a cracker,' he said. 'That husband of yours doesn't appreciate what he's got!'

'I'm sure he does,' Claire came back, trying for a light note. 'I really should get back, Tony. It's half past twelve already.'

'What's the rush? He isn't home tonight, is he?'

'No, but ...'

'Well then.' He stood up, drawing her to her feet. 'Come and dance first. Just for a few minutes.'

Claire cast a glance in Dinah's direction, but the older woman had her face pressed into her husband's shoulder, her fingers playing with the hair at the nape of his neck while his rested heavily on her hips. She had the feeling that any request to be taken home would only be met with laughing derision from that quarter.

'All right, a few minutes,' she agreed with reluctance. 'But then I really shall have to go.'

Tony didn't answer, drawing her into his arms and starting to move very slowly in time to the music. He was holding her too close and Claire didn't like what was happening, but when she attempted to draw away he wouldn't let her.

'Come on, baby,' he murmured, smiling down into her eyes. 'Be your age!'

Dinah and Reg had come to a stop by the door to the hall. Now Dinah reached out a hand to open it, holding on to her husband with the other. 'We're going up,' she announced baldly. 'Enjoy yourselves, you two.'

There was a silence in the room after the two had gone. Claire listened numbly to the sound of feet climbing the staircase, a high tinkle of laughter and the thud of a door closing somewhere upstairs. Tony was watching her, his arms still around her back. After a moment he let her go.

'You're not playing, are you?' he said flatly. 'I should have known you weren't the type.'

Claire looked at him with directness. 'Did Dinah give you the impression I might be?'

'Not in so many words,' he conceded. 'Just something ...' He broke off, shrugged his shoulders. 'No sweat. There's plenty of it around.' Meeting her eyes, he had the grace to look faintly abashed. 'Sorry, I didn't mean to say that. I'd better take you home.'

'I'd be okay in a taxi,' she said, and saw his expression change.

'You'll be safe enough, don't worry. I know when I've struck out. You didn't have a coat, did you?'

Claire shook her head. After the amount Tony had drunk she would still prefer a taxi, although he seemed perfectly sober.

'You'll have to say goodnight to Dinah and Reg for me,' she said uncomfortably on the way out, and knew then that she would not be seeing the other woman again.

They had little to say to one another on the way across the silent town. Tired and miserable, Claire could only think longingly of bed and sweet oblivion. Come tomorrow she would have to start sorting herself out, but for now she wanted just to forget.

The sight of Rod's car parked on the driveway when they turned the corner brought a gasp of dismay to her lips. What on earth was he doing home? He had taken an overnight bag, hadn't he? She couldn't have made a mistake about that!

'Husband?' Tony asked unnecessarily.

'Yes,' she acknowledged, dry-throated. 'He must have changed his mind about staying over.'

'Want me to come in with you and explain where you were?'

The offer was made with reluctance. If he knew Rod he wouldn't have made it at all, she reflected without humour. She saw a figure appear in the lighted sitting room window and hastily opened her door.

'The best thing you can do is go,' she said. 'Thanks for bringing me home.'

'My pleasure.' He sounded glad to be out of it. 'Good luck.'

Rod opened the front door as she came up the path, eyes going beyond her to the disappearing tail lights of the car. His face was set and hard, the grey eyes like steel.

'Where the hell do you think you've been?' he demanded. 'I was just about to start phoning the police!'

'I went out with the Shaws,' Claire told him with what composure she could muster. 'That was Dinah's brother Tony who just brought me home.'

'And couldn't find time to stop and say hallo.'

'I told him not to,' she said. 'It wasn't his fault I went out tonight.'

'But his fault you stayed out, I'll bet. What did you do, park on some lane?'

They were inside the house with the door closed against the night, but there was precious little comfort in the wall at her back. Face pale, Claire said huskily, 'I'm not going to demean myself even trying to deny that. Believe what you want to. I'm going to bed.'

The hand which seized her bruised her flesh. 'Not until I say so.'

Claire found herself propelled ahead of him into the sitting room and pushed into a chair while he went to close the curtains. Remembering the lock on the spare room door, she had a strong urge to make a run for it, but pride held her back. Her conscience was clear no matter what Rod believed. She wasn't going to let him browbeat her in any way.

'You just couldn't wait, could you,' he said bitingly, turning back to her. 'Not two months married and I can't even trust you to spend one night on your own!'

'I've spent the last four on my own,' she pointed out, and saw his lips thin anew.

'By your own choice. You're not going to use sex as a lever to get your own way with me.' He paused, his regard cold. 'I decided to come back tonight so we could spend tomorrow getting straightened out.'

'Really?' Claire's gaze was equally unflinching. 'Are you sure it wasn't because Pauline turned you down?'

Even as she said it she was already regretting it, but it was too late for retractions. His face had gone quite blank except for the sudden, frightening glitter in his eyes.

'If frustration is all you think I'm suffering from there's one good remedy,' he muttered, and began taking off his jacket.

His tie had followed it before Claire could get her limbs to move. She came unsteadily to her feet, letting out a small cry of protest as he reached for her. 'Rod, no!'

She might as well have appealed to a brick wall for all the response she got. She was wearing only flimsy briefs and bra under the trouser suit. He took those off too, handling her with a total lack of tenderness like some shop window dummy.

Dropped on to the sofa cushions, Claire made one last attempt to get through to him, pressing her hands frantically against his shoulders as he knelt over her. 'Rod, please! Not like this!'

'Just like this,' he said harshly. 'It's what you need.'

'No.' It was little more than a moan this time, her body racked by the dry sobs tearing the lining of her throat. 'Oh, God, don't!'

He went still, his teeth gritted together, his hands hurting her with the sheer increase of pressure as he forcibly brought himself under control. Then she was free and he was gone, her clothing left where he had dropped it on the floor. The slam of the bedroom door shook the whole house.

It was some time before Claire could force herself to get up. She felt icy cold and couldn't stop shivering, although the room itself was warm enough. Somehow she managed to pull on a couple of garments and gather up the rest. Her mind was empty of everything but the one thought. Rod had almost raped her. Could anything she had said or done have asked for that?

The main bedroom door was firmly closed against her when she finally dragged herself upstairs. Not that she would have contemplated entering it had it been otherwise. They were finished. After tonight there could be no other solution. Rod couldn't have treated her like that if he loved her. He had never loved her, not the way she wanted him to. She only wished she never had to see him again.

That wasn't possible, of course. He was already down when she came into the kitchen at seven-thirty after a sleepless night. He looked surprisingly normal, she thought dispassionately, letting her glance slide over him as he looked up from the breakfast bar where he was drinking coffee. For a monster, that was.

'Claire,' he said quietly, 'we have to talk.'

'I don't want to talk,' she said, taking milk from the refrigerator. 'Not to you.'

He watched her pour the milk into a saucepan and add water before tapping the percolator at his elbow. 'There's plenty in here.'

'I'll make my own, thanks.'

The sigh was long and drawn-out. 'Now you're being childish. Not that that should surprise me. You never did grow up.'

'I suppose if I had I'd have accepted what you tried to do last night without complaint,' she retorted with contempt. 'I'll never forgive you for that!'

'I'm not proud of it.' There was a pause and a change of tone. 'Like it or not, we're going to have to talk it out. What happened last night was nasty and I'm not trying to find excuses, but ...'

'Because there aren't any,' she flashed, rounding on him. 'And you know it!'

'All right, there aren't any.' He was holding on to his temper with an obvious effort. 'I should have treated you the way I'd treat any other deserving brat. What you seem to be forgetting is that it didn't happen in the end.'

'You think what you did wasn't enough?' She quivered,

remembering. 'You deliberately humiliated me!'

'I've seen you without clothes before.'

'You know what I mean.'

The irony went from his eyes. He shrugged resignedly. 'I could say I'm sorry from now till Christmas and it wouldn't alter anything. If we're going to work things out we have to accept last night the way it was.'

Claire shook her head. 'We're not going to work things out. We're not even going to try.' She took a slow breath, only now acknowledging what had been in her mind for hours. 'I'm going home to Meadowbank, and Bill.'

Rod's expression didn't change. 'That might be difficult. He's coming here tomorrow evening. I'm to pick him up in Layburn at eight.'

She stared at him in dismay. 'You invited my father here!'

'Call it half and half. He wanted to come and I saw no reason why he shouldn't.'

'Even knowing the way things were with us?'

'I'd counted on you having enough regard for him to put personal problems to one side for the present.'

'I might have been able to do that before, but now ...' Claire firmed her voice ... 'you'll have to phone through and put him off.'

'Telling him what?'

'Whatever you like. You'll think of something.'

'We could try the truth,' Rod suggested on a dry note. 'If it's sympathy you're looking for, that might do the trick. Tell him what a hardhearted louse of a man you married and what a big mistake it's all been—if you can bear to admit to having made it.'

Thinking back on the number of times Bill had expressed doubts on the depth of her feelings for Rod, Claire knew she couldn't bear it. An obsession, he had called it, and he had been right. She had been obsessed with the idea of marrying Rod, of laying claim to a man others had been unable to tie down, without giving herself time to get to know him in any real sense of the word. His dominance had been a novelty—exciting to play with but impossible to live with. Even if she were prepared to compromise he would not.

'It would hardly be fair to bring him into it,' she said stiffly at length. 'Can't you just make out it isn't as convenient as you thought right now?'

'You think he wouldn't guess something was wrong?' Rod shook his head. 'I'm not even going to attempt it. So far as I'm concerned, he's welcome. And if you think anything of him at all, you'll shelve our differences until he's gone.'

He had her in a cleft stick and he knew it. There was nothing else Claire could do but agree under the circumstances.

'Only don't think this alters anything,' she added fiercely. 'Once he's gone back I'm leaving you, Rod.'

'We'll have to try for the Guinness Book of Records,' he retorted with sardonic inflection. 'Although I suppose there'll be shorter marriages on record.' He came to his feet, the movement abrupt. 'Not much point in my hanging around. I may as well go up to the site.'

'By all means. Mustn't neglect the job!'

He paused in the doorway to look back at her, expression controlled. 'If you meant what you said you'd better watch yourself. I don't have anything to lose, do I?'

Claire sat down heavily after he had gone. Nothing to lose. Nothing except a situation he hadn't particularly wanted to get into in the first place. Perhaps he was even relieved underneath.

She wasn't sure what her own true feelings were. Right at this moment she wasn't sure about anything any more.

CHAPTER NINE

IT was good to see her father again despite the circumstances. He looked well, she thought.

Difficulties she had not foreseen about this visit included her return to a shared bedroom in order to keep the impression of marital harmony going. Restful sleep was hard to come by while trying to keep a gap down the middle of a double bed. After wakening the second morning to find herself curled up against Rod's side with his arm heavy across her waist, Claire tried to solve the problem with a pillow between the two of them, drawing nothing but silent derision from the other side of it. It worked anyway, saving her from the alternative of spending her nights wrapped in a blanket on the floor. Rod himself obviously having no intention of vacating the bed.

'You know you're being quite ridiculous,' he said once.

Claire did know, but she couldn't stop it. Something in her drove her to emphasise her rejection of him in every way possible when they were alone—perhaps to make up for the act she had to put on when they were not, she reasoned. One thing she did know: the latter was becoming harder and harder to keep up. Sooner or later Bill had to guess all was not as it should be between them. He couldn't fail to guess.

If he did suspect he kept his own counsel on the subject. The weekend over, he showed no signs of wanting to return to London, accompanying Rod out to the site most mornings and returning to the house for lunch. Sunny afternoons he spent out on the patio, stretched full length on a lounger with a newspaper over his face.

'The first real rest I've had in years,' he admitted to Claire one such afternoon when she brought out tea for them both. 'I'll have to start delegating more.' There was a pause before he added on a different note, 'I've been thinking about offering Rod that partnership.'

Claire's head jerked. She didn't dare look at her father. 'Just because he's your son-in-law?' she made herself ask.

'Not wholly. He's one of the best engineers in the field, and he knows as much about the business as I do. That's a fair recommendation, wouldn't you say?'

'Very.' Her next question was harder to ask. 'Does he know about it?'

'We haven't discussed it directly, but he must have some idea. It was one reason for coming north this week.'

Which explained Rod's reluctance to cancel the visit, Claire thought with cynicism. For the first time she began to wonder about his motives in marrying her at all. Had she been the real attraction?

'You've been here five days,' she pointed out, already knowing the answer. 'I'd have thought if you'd been going to talk it over you'd have done it by now.'

'Yes, I would,' he agreed. 'Except that I thought it better to wait till whatever it is between you two had blown over.'

She looked at him then, a swift glance which took in the question in his eyes. 'You guessed, then.'

'It's impossible to miss the tension between you when you're together. Just a fairly normal difference of opinions, I thought, when I first arrived, but it's more than that, isn't it?'

Claire nodded unhappily. 'I'm afraid so. We're incompatible.'

'How?'

'Temperament. Rod wants everything his way and I'm not prepared to accept it.'

Her father smiled faintly. 'Are you sure he wants everything his way, or could it be just that he won't let you have it all yours?'

'You don't know him ...' she began, but he waved her down.

'Oh, yes, I do. Better than you seem to. I knew there'd be trouble ahead if you married him, but you would do it. You'll just have to learn how to handle him, that's all.'

'You mean by giving in?'

'Not necessarily.' He studied her a moment and sighed. 'It's a pity you never knew your mother. She could have taught you a whole lot about strategy. If there was something she particularly wanted me to do, and I refused to play, she'd simply bide her time, then approach the whole subject from another angle. Quite often I'd find myself doing something I thought was my own idea till I'd catch a certain expression in her eye and realise the connection.'

'Why should she have had to go to all that trouble?' Claire demanded.

'Because she loved me,' he said softly. 'Enough to indulge my ego a little. Where a man's concerned it's wrapped up with pride. Strip him of it and he's not a man any longer, not in his own estimation.'

'What about a woman's pride?'

'Not the same thing.'

'You mean you men like to think it isn't. Mine is just as important to me as Rod's is to him!'

He looked resigned. 'If you really believe that there's no way I can help. You're going to have to sort things out for yourself.'

'I'm not sure I want to,' she admitted, and saw his gaze sharpen.

'Claire, you've been married to the man less than two months. You can't be tired of him already!'

'It isn't a case of being tired of him. I told you, we're ...'

'Incompatible. Yes, I heard the first time.' He sounded impatient. 'There's more to incompatibility than a clash of wills. I don't know what this particular fall-out was about, and I don't want to know, but you were okay up until then, weren't you?'

'No,' she denied with vehemence. 'No, we weren't! He thinks more about the job than he does about me.'

'Ah, now we're really coming down to it. The same old cry. When are you women going to realise that a man's job is a major part of his life? If he's no interest in what he's doing that's the real tragedy.'

'There's a difference between interest and obsession! I hardly ever see him.'

'He comes home at night, doesn't he?'

'Only just.'

'Well, if you show your resentment the way you're showing it now it's hardly surprising.' He shook his head. 'Claire, you're asking too much. Rod had till November to get the first stage completed and it's going to be tight. After that things will start to slacken off some.'

'After that it will be too late,' she came back stubbornly. 'He's managing the project, not building it physically himself. He could delegate authority to the resident engineer.'

'Whose function is to see that the job is completed to specification, not worry about the actual construction work, as you very well know. There are snags likely to crop up every day, modifications to be made—a thousand and one things that can go wrong. Rod has to be on the spot to deal with them as and when they occur, not God knows where entertaining his wife! And don't try telling me you'd be content to sit around here with him if he were at home more, because you wouldn't.'

'I shan't try telling you anything,' Claire retorted. 'You and Rod are too much alike!'

'You knew that before you married him. The truth is you closed your mind to it because it might have meant not having him at all.' Bill's tone softened suddenly. 'Claire, try and see reason. If you love one another that's all that matters in the long run.'

'That's just it,' she said huskily. 'I'm not sure we do. I think it was mainly physical for both of us.'

'So what? It often is to start with. You're not giving it the chance to turn into anything deeper.' His smile was reminiscent. 'Marriage doesn't come perfect overnight, it takes time and perseverance. A baby might give you more to think about.'

'I'm not having one just for that reason,' she stated flatly. 'Anyway ...' She broke off, biting her lip. After a moment she said on a low note. 'When you go I'd like to come home with you to Meadowbank.'

It was a moment before he replied, and when he did his own tone held an almost apologetic note. 'Meadowbank isn't your home any longer. It won't even be mine for very much longer. I've got a pretty certain buyer.'

'You've sold the house!'

'I do have the right,' dryly. 'It was too big for the two of us. For just me it's ridiculous. I don't entertain since you left.'

Claire controlled any further protests with an effort. 'But it will be some time before you're actually ready to sign contracts,' she pointed out. 'I could come till then.'

'No.' There was no mistaking the unequivocal note in his voice. 'I'm not taking any kind of part in this. If you want to leave Rod, you do it under your own steam.'

'Thanks,' she said bitterly. 'I can't even rely on my own father to help!'

The accusation failed to move him appreciably. 'I am helping. I'm giving you the chance to think it over. If you run out on Rod you might not get a second chance.'

'If I leave him it will be because I don't want a second chance!' She stopped abruptly, added on a quieter note, 'I'm sorry if this ruins your plans for a partnership.'

'From my point of view, it doesn't,' Bill responded with a firming of his jaw. 'I need somebody I can trust and rely on to take some of the load, somebody younger with the right experience. Rod is the only one I know who meets all the qualifications.'

Claire looked at him in disbelief. 'What about me? Don't my feelings count at all?'

'Of course they count.'

'But not as much as your business interests.'

He shook his head a little impatiently. 'They're two separate things. Don't resort to emotional blackmail, Claire, it's unworthy of you.'

'As considering what you are considering after what I've told you is unworthy of you,' she retorted on a hard note. 'What makes you think he'd accept anyway?'

'He might not. If you can make him feel guilty enough he almost certainly won't.'

'Meaning I'd be depriving him of a fine opportunity by leaving him.'

Her father paused before answering, obviously searching for the right words. 'I think you'd be depriving yourself of something more valuable,' he said at last. 'That last night I saw the two of you in town, I'd have said you had something worth hanging on to. Things can't have changed so radically in the space of a few weeks.'

Things could, Claire reflected painfully, because they had. Rod had proved himself less than the man she thought he was.

She let the subject drop after that, feeling tense and

miserable. If there was a chance of moving from this place in the near future it might help matters, but the thought of spending a whole winter here was more than she could bear. Partnership or not, Rod would want to see this job out. So why not try offering him an ultimatum? Claire asked herself. The job, or her. That should sort out his priorities. There were others who could take over here.

In the light of her father's awareness, Claire made less of an attempt to dissemble that evening, answering when Rod spoke to her directly but otherwise remaining silent. Once or twice as the two men talked together, she found herself appraising the man she had married with a stranger's detachment, seeing the character lines etched about mouth and eyes, the stubborn jut of his jaw. To do him justice, he had warned her that his ideas of a wife's place were neither modern nor progressive, but she hadn't really believed it. There had to be more to her role than preparing his meals, cleaning his clothes, sharing his bed.

Because it was such a fine night they had eaten outdoors. Claire left them there chatting while she went to load the dishwasher, thinking of the evenings at Meadowbank when she had had nothing more strenuous to do after a meal than read a book or take a stroll, when some more exciting pursuit did not beckon. If she had married Peter life would have been fun still—something different every day. A service flat in town would have taken all the drudgery out of being married.

But could Peter St John have roused the kind of feelings Rod had stirred in her? asked a small voice somewhere at the back of her mind. Could any other man have done that? Claire steeled herself against the sudden flood of longing which swept her. The issue went deeper than mere sexual gratification. She mustn't allow that to cloud things.

That was easier said than done, she found, lying on her

side of the bed later that night while Rod undressed. She wanted to feel his arms about her again the way they used to be, the pressure of his lips laying claim. The deprivation seemed to bother him little. Could he have already been tiring of her before all this happened? she began to wonder, and felt concern spring alive at the thought.

The silence stretched after he was in bed with the light out. He had drawn the curtains back far enough to cast shadows on the wall. Claire watched them until she could bear it no longer.

'Did Bill offer you a partnership tonight?' she asked unevenly.

If the question had taken him by surprise it wasn't evident from his calm reply. 'Yes, he did.'

Claire waited until it became obvious that nothing further was forthcoming. Finally, she was forced into saying it, 'Well?'

'I said I'd think it over.' There was still no particular inflection in his voice.

She hesitated, then, 'Because of us?' she made herself ask at last.

'I'd say it was a fair reason, wouldn't you?'

'I suppose so.' Her throat hurt.

'There's no suppose about it. If you're intent on keeping this up there isn't much point in considering any kind of permanent arrangement.'

'You started it,' she pointed out with some asperity, and heard his impatient release of breath.

'I didn't start anything. I lost my temper and nearly did something I'd have regretted afterwards, but we'd have been over that now if you'd been willing to meet me halfway over the whole affair. You still believe you were the injured party, don't you?'

Her voice came low. 'No, not altogether. I shouldn't have said what I did.'

'About what?'

'About Pauline.'

His laugh was grim. 'You really think that's what got my goat?'

'Wasn't it?'

Rod came up on one elbow to look at her across the bulk of the pillow between them, dark head silhouetted against the window. 'If I thought you were stringing me along ...' he threatened.

'I'm not.' Claire lay quite still gazing up at him, heart thudding like a trip-hammer. 'I shouldn't have gone off with Dinah that night either. Is that what you're waiting to hear?'

'It's the brother who concerns me more,' he came back harshly. 'Or did, at any rate.'

The contraction was sudden and painful. 'Does that mean you don't care any more?'

The reply seemed a long time coming. She couldn't see his eyes because his back was to the only available source of light.

'That rather depends on you,' he said at length. 'Do you want me to care?'

He was putting it firmly back in her lap and there was no way she could wriggle out of it. If she said no as pride prompted, then this whole conversation had been a total waste of time. On the other hand, if she said yes, it implied more than she was sure she felt herself.

Rod was minus his pyjama jacket as usual, and the gleam of moonlight caught the top of his shoulders, making the skin shine. Without pausing to think about it, Claire put out a hand and touched the swell of his bicep, feeling the hardness beneath her fingers with a surging of emotion which overrode doubt.

'Yes,' she whispered.

The pillow vanished, slung from the bed in one abrupt

movement as he came to her. There was little tenderness in his mouth, but it wasn't tenderness she sought. He should have done this before, she thought in the fleeting moment before her senses overwhelmed her. What did anything matter compared with what was happening now?

It was only later, when rationality had returned, that she acknowledged how far from being solved the problem was. The head at present cradled on her shoulder held a mind she still had to reach. She could tell from Rod's breathing that he wasn't asleep. Rod never did go to sleep right after making love as she believed some men did. Most times he would hold her until she slept.

She said softly now, 'Rod, if you do decide to accept Bill's offer, couldn't you put someone else in charge of this job?'

For a moment there was no reaction. When he did move it was slowly, head lifting to look at her.

'Is that the price?'

She winced at his tone but refused to be put down. 'It's just a question.'

'Asked at what might be considered the strategic moment,' he said on a hard note of irony. 'You should have made it just before, not after.'

'I didn't ...' she began, but he stopped her with a hand over her mouth, leaving it there heavily.

'Don't make a liar of yourself into the bargain. No, I wouldn't be putting in anyone else. What I start I finish.'

'I won't stay here!' she whispered fiercely when he took his hand away. 'I hate this place!'

'That's up to you.' He sounded tired. 'I can't make you stay.'

'But if I go you won't come with me.'

'No.' He moved away from her. 'Do you want me to put the pillow back?'

Claire didn't answer. There was nothing left to say. If

Rod wouldn't consider doing as she asked at a time like this he was hardly likely to change his mind in the cold light of day. She was left with two choices: back down or back out. Neither held any attraction.

It was half past eight when she awoke. Rod was gone from the bed and she could hear no sound from downstairs, although he didn't normally leave before nine. Memory brought a flush to her cheeks. He could hardly be blamed for believing her response to him pure calculation on her part. To a certain extent it might have been at first, if she were honest, but not for long. In Rod's arms it was possible to forget everything outside of the moment.

Her father's room door was standing ajar. Probably he had gone with Rod again. He would know why Rod was hesitating, of course, and he would be blaming her. Yet why shouldn't she be allocated some consideration too? At least Rod had work to occupy his mind. What did she have?

There was an envelope propped against the coffee percolator where she would be sure to see it. Claire took it up and extracted the single sheet of paper it contained with memories of another time. As before, it was right to the point:

I'm going back today to give you and Rod a chance to sort yourselves out on your own. If you let selfishness come between you, you don't know what love is about. Have you thought about finding yourself some kind of job to pass the time on? Even in Colwood there must be something you could do.

Such as what? Claire wondered dismally, looking out of the window to the high fells. One term at commercial college barely fitted her for anything likely to be found round here. She paused there as a thought struck her. Unless she offered her services to Rod out at the site office. There was a clerk of some kind already, she knew, but he would probably be more than glad of the help. Relatively low as her typing speed must be by now, it would soon pick up again with a little practice.

The more she considered the idea the more she liked the sound of it. The ideal solution. Not even an extra on overheads, because she wouldn't be on salary. At the very least she could learn enough about the job to be able to discuss it intelligently with Rod on occasion, and that could hardly do their marriage any harm.

Coming in at six to the savoury smell of cooking, Rod looked surprised and somewhat wary. Considering the strain between them last night, Claire could see why he might wonder what she was up to now. She still felt bad about the way she had approached the subject, but tonight should help to make up for it.

She had a Martini ready for him when he came down after his shower, mixed just the way he liked it with plenty of ice.

'Supper in ten minutes,' she said, taking a sip from her own glass as he lounged in a chair close by the open patio doors. 'It's a lot cooler tonight.'

'It's autumn,' he said. His eyes following the shape of her in the softly flowing russet leisure gown. 'I haven't seen you wear that since our honeymoon.'

'I remembered you liked it.' She paused before adding softly, 'I'm sorry about last night, Rod.'

He smiled faintly. 'When last night?'

'Afterwards.' Claire felt her lips corresponding. 'I didn't mean what I said about leaving you.'

'I'm glad to hear it.' Rod put down his glass and stretched out a hand to her, the grey eyes still veiled. 'Come here, Claire.'

She went quickly, dropping to her knees on the floor at his side with her fingers enfolded in that strong, secure grasp. His kiss was briefer than she had anticipated, and she seemed to sense in it an odd quality of reserve, yet his expression suggested no undercurrents when he raised his head again.

'You don't seem too concerned over Bill leaving so suddenly,' he remarked.

'I'm not,' she said. 'Oh, I've missed him, of course, but it's nice to have the place to ourselves again.' Her eyes were bright. 'He left me a note. Suggested I should find something to occupy my mind more.'

Rod lifted a quizzical brow. 'Any ideas as to what?'

'Yes, but I'll tell you about it later.' She pressed herself lightly to her feet. 'I still have one or two things to finish in the kitchen.'

They ate at seven by the light of the slowly setting sun. Afterwards, Claire insisted Rod take his brandy and a cigar back to the sitting room while she went to make coffee. He was occupying the same chair, though with the patio doors now closed when she carried through the tray, the cigar smouldering between his fingers.

'All right,' he said resignedly watching her pour. 'What are you setting me up for this time?'

The note in his voice brought her head up a little sharply, but she managed to control the impulsive retort. He had every excuse for being suspicious, she supposed.

'It isn't setting up so much as making up,' she said. 'I haven't been much of a wife to you these last couple of weeks, have I?'

His smile was dry. 'Things could have been better.'

'They will be,' Claire promised. 'They really will!' She paused, looking for the right words, wanting to communicate her enthusiasm to him. 'Rod, I want to come and work for you up at the site. I realise you already have somebody in the office, but I'm sure there must be plenty I can do. At least I wouldn't be complaining that I hardly ever see you.' The animation faded a little as she registered his expression. 'Don't you think it's a good idea?'

'No,' he said, 'I don't.'

She gazed at him in dismay, barely able to support the sense of let-down. 'Why?' she got out at last.

'Two reasons.' He sounded almost brusque about it. 'One, the amount of clerical work calls for only one assistant, and we already have a very capable one, as you pointed out, and two...' he hesitated a moment as if he were also searching for the right words, then apparently decided that the only way to say it was bluntly ... 'I don't believe in husband and wife spending all their time in each other's pockets. If you feel you must have a job of some kind I won't stand in your way, although I have to admit I don't like it very much either.'

'Doing what?' she asked dully.

'Whatever's available, I imagine—within reason.'

'Fine. I happen to know Mary Cawthorne's husband needs a couple of new bricklayers.'

His lips thinned. 'If you feel like that we'll shelve the whole subject.'

'How do you expect me to feel?' Claire was sitting forward in her seat, body tensed, eyes dark. 'You just got through telling me you don't want to see me for more than a couple of hours or so a day.'

'That wasn't what I said.'

'It's what you implied.'

He gave a sudden sigh, leaning forward to stub out the remainder of the cigar in the nearest ashtray. 'It wasn't what I implied either. I meant exactly what I said. I don't want my wife working for me, with me or anything else in that line. If you want the truth, I don't want a working wife at all. It wasn't what I married you for.'

'What was?' she demanded bitterly.

'I'm beginning to wonder.' He was in control of himself and all the more hurtful because of it. 'I should have known there was absolutely no hope of you changing.'

'Why should I change?'

'Because you need to grow up.'

'If being adult in your estimation means accepting the kind of life style we have here I won't bother, thanks. What you needed was a doormat, not a wife, someone who'd be waiting every night when you came home, all wide-eyed and worshipping!'

'It sounds close,' he responded with irony. 'I warned you my ideas were old-fashioned.'

Her lips curled. 'They're not old-fashioned, they're antediluvian. Except when it comes to lovemaking. You want the best of both worlds, Rod.'

'You're so right.' Grey eyes glinted cruelly. 'And I finish up with neither!'

The hurt went deep, but nothing would have persuaded her to show it. 'Perhaps I should take a leaf out of your book and try a little variety,' she retaliated. 'They say only practice makes perfect.'

His anger faded suddenly, leaving a hint of self-disgust. 'Let's leave it there, shall we? We've both said too much. If you want to take a job, do it. Just don't expect me to like it, that's all.'

He picked up a newspaper, shutting her out in a way which left nothing more to be said. Trembling, Claire got up and left him there, going through to the darkened kitchen to lean her hot forehead against a cool bit of wall and try to sort out her emotions. If she had loved Rod once she certainly didn't now. He was hateful. If only she had waited—given herself time to know him better before rushing into marriage. Yet would it have made any real difference? One had to live with a person to know them at all.

One thing she could do now that Bill was gone was move back into the other room. After what Rod had said a few minutes ago she had no intention of sharing a bed with him again. Let him find himself someone who could fulfil all his requirements, as no doubt Pauline Barton had. He should have married her instead; she would have been willing enough.

She had been in bed over an hour before Rod came up. There was a brief pause after he opened their door, then the sound of purposeful footsteps coming back along the landing. He came straight in and across to the bed, tossing back the clothes to scoop her bodily out of it.

'I'm not living this way,' he said grimly. 'Like it or not, we're married and we're staying married!'

Tossed none too gently on to the double bed a moment later, Claire said on a low note, 'You're going to have to use force, Rod. There's no way you could make me want you again.'

His glance was belittling. 'I'm not even going to try. Right now, I've no desire to try.'

'Then why bring me back in here at all?' she flashed at him.

'Because it's where you belong.'

'Even knowing how I feel about you?'

He slid off his shirt without bothering to turn his head this time. 'I don't know how you feel about me; I don't think you know yourself. One thing I do know, sulking in another room isn't going to help matters.'

'Nothing is going to help matters,' Claire acknowledged, tone gone suddenly flat. 'When I try to take an interest in your job you throw it back in my face.'

'I already explained my reasons. Apart from anything else, Judy is more than capable of doing the job on her own. How do you think she'd feel if I agreed to what you were suggesting? There's no way I'd be able to convince her it wasn't because I found her inadequate.'

Claire was barely listening. Her eyes were fixed on him. 'I thought all the site employees were male.'

'There's no hard and fast rule. It depends on circumstances. I'd hardly take a lone female along on a job like the last one, for instance.' His lips twisted. 'Once was enough.'

'You didn't take me,' she said. 'I was sent.'

'I didn't have to keep you there.'

'*I* wish you hadn't too. I'd have been married to Peter now instead of you!'

Rod finished pulling on his pyjama trousers before looking at her, the lean features devoid of expression. 'He had a lucky escape.'

'Swine,' she said bitterly. 'I should have expected that from you.'

'You get what you ask for. I'm not too good at turning the other cheek.'

Claire lay still as he left the room. There came the sound of water running, muffled by the walls between. Her chest felt tight with sheer aching misery. They couldn't go on like this. They just couldn't! Rod hated her as much as she hated him. What was the use?

He made no attempt to touch her when he did come to bed, but neither did he stick so rigorously to his own side of it as Claire was intent on doing. The pillow would be a wasted gesture, she knew; he was in no mood to tolerate it. Ridiculous anyway, she acknowledged wryly. Childish, just as he had said.

The tears came without warning, jerking sobs which tore at her throat. She tried to stifle them in the pillow, but it was useless. Beside her, Rod sighed and turned, bringing her round towards him and holding her.

'Don't,' he said. 'We'll work it out.'

There was comfort in the feel of his arms despite everything else. It was only gradually that she became aware of something missing.

'You don't even want me any more, do you?' she

whispered painfully, and heard another sigh.

'Not right now, no. I'm tired.'

'Of me?'

'Don't be silly.' He eased his embrace, allowing her to roll back into the crook of his arm. 'We both have some adjusting to do, that's all. Go to sleep, Claire. There's always tomorrow.'

She lay awake long after he had fallen asleep, trying to see light at the end of the tunnel. No amount of adjustment was going to bring back what they had had at the start, she acknowledged fatalistically in the end. All they could hope for was a compromise of sorts, and that wasn't going to make either of them happy. Thinking back to what her father had said the day before, she knew in her heart that there was only one way back. If she wanted Rod *she* had to be prepared to make the sacrifices. What she had to decide was did she want him enough.

CHAPTER TEN

CLAIRE had heard nothing from Dinah since the night Tony had brought her home. Bumping into the other woman in town one morning proved mildly embarrassing until Dinah herself removed the awkwardness by frankly apologising for any misunderstanding.

'I'd had too much to drink,' she said, 'and I knew our Tone was fancying you like mad. I suppose I was thinking more of him than you.' Her glance rested speculatively on Claire's face. 'Come and have a coffee in Maces. It'll pass half an hour along.'

Claire went because she had nothing better to do. Any company was better than none. In any case, she couldn't dislike Dinah. There was something about her which defied dislike.

One coffee became two, and finally extended into lunch at the Copper Kettle, which was Colwood's best restaurant. They were lucky to get a table without a reservation on market day, but Dinah was on friendly terms with the manageress and managed to secure a last-minute cancellation.

'You know, you're not the same person I knew a few weeks ago,' she remarked candidly while they waited for their order to arrive. 'You've lost all your sparkle. Isn't marriage all you thought it might be?'

Claire smiled faintly. 'Is it ever?'

'For some maybe. I suppose it depends on just how much you do expect.'

'Did you? Expect a lot, I mean.'

'Oh, sure. I got most of it too—eventually. It took some pushing, though.'

'I didn't mean so much in the material sense,' said Claire carefully. 'You said once that you only came to live out here because Reg wanted to.'

'Yes, he always had a thing about getting away from it all when he could afford it.'

'And you don't mind?'

'Not enough to make a song and dance about it.' Dinah smiled and shrugged. 'There's always plenty of light relief available if I get downhearted. Don't look so shocked. There might come a time when you start looking round too.'

'I wasn't shocked,' Claire denied. 'Just wondering.' She paused before adding bluntly, 'Did you ever make a pass at Rod, Dinah?'

The smile didn't falter. 'Is that what he told you?'

'Yes.'

'Then he must be right, though I can't remember the exact moment. It's second nature to me, love. Nine times out of ten it doesn't mean a thing.'

Claire didn't believe her, but it wasn't important. Rod's fidelity was one thing she didn't have to worry about. He worked far too hard to have the time.

The doorbell tinkled as someone else entered the restaurant. Dinah was facing in that direction. Her expression underwent a sudden change.

'Talking of the devil,' she murmured. 'Your husband just walked in. No, don't turn round. He hasn't seen us.'

Claire hadn't attempted to turn her head. Surprise was uppermost in her mind. What would Rod be doing here in town in the middle of the day? He normally ate out at the site.

'It hardly matters if he does see us,' she said. 'They can always lay another place.'

'Two places.' There was an odd note to Dinah's voice. 'He has someone with him.'

Claire gazed at her for several seconds before realisation dawned. She felt her own face go blank. 'Who?' she managed.

'Her name is Judy Blackstock—or Woods, as she prefers to be known now. She got a divorce three months ago.' Something in Dinah seemed almost to be enjoying the situation. 'I wonder how he met her?'

'I think she works in the site office,' said Claire. Her mind felt numb. Until a couple of weeks ago she hadn't even known Rod employed a woman in any capacity, and now here he was lunching her in town. The first time? She doubted it. It explained so much about his attitude. When he bothered to make love to her at all these days it was in a purely physical sense, as if performing a duty. She had blamed herself for being unable to produce any depth of response. Now she suddenly wasn't so sure. 'What's she like?' she heard herself asking.

'Fair-haired, attractive—she always was. Someone said she'd got a new job a while back, but I didn't realise where. Your father must pay good rates. She needs the money with two kids to keep. From what I heard, Frank pays maintenance when he feels like it. Rotten situation to be in at her age. She can't be more than twenty-six.'

A part of Claire wanted to tell Dinah to shut up, another part needed to hear more. She wished she dared turn round and see for herself, but she was too afraid of what she might see.

'Don't take it to heart,' Dinah advised, watching her. 'It's probably all quite innocent—although you'd have thought he might have contacted you if he knew he was going to be in town for lunch today. Still, it could have been a last-minute arrangement.'

The arrival of their soup curtailed conversation for a

moment or two. Claire stared at her plate without attempting to pick up her spoon. She had never felt less like eating in her life. She wanted to get up and go, but with the meal ordered on Dinah's bill how could she? She had to sit here for at least another half an hour, knowing her husband was just across the room with another woman. Innocent or not, he had never found the time to bring her here for lunch during the week. That alone was enough.

Somehow she got through the meal, picking at each dish with scanty appetite and stifling a protest when Dinah ordered more coffee. All she wanted to do was to get home and be on her own to think.

'You can relax,' said Dinah over the rim of her cup a few minutes later. 'They're leaving. He's still not looking in this direction.'

Claire was thankful for that. She doubted herself capable of carrying off the kind of situation which might have occurred. She caught a fleeting glimpse of a fair-haired young woman in a grey trouser suit through the mirror hung on the wall in front of her, confirmed as the one she sought by the equally fleeting appearance of Rod's familiar figure a step behind. The door opened and closed again, and they were gone.

'There you are, you see. A hurried business lunch.' Dinah sounded cheerfully reassuring. 'Nothing to worry about.'

'Except that they had no business being here,' Claire met the other woman's eyes across the table with control. 'You could see them all the time. Don't fob me off with half truths. Was it impersonal?'

Dinah hesitated. 'Well, he did hold her hand a couple of times. It could have meant anything or nothing. What are you going to do about it anyway?'

'Nothing,' Claire said flatly. 'What can I do?'

'Not a lot,' Dinah admitted. 'Not without proof. If he

doesn't mention it to you I'd say that constituted proof enough.'

Claire doubted if he would regardless, but refrained from saying so. There was no point in airing the fact that they were already so far apart.

She took her leave of Dinah with relief. Once in the car, however, she headed not for the house but out in the other direction towards the dam. There was a wild beauty in the sweeping, heather-clad moorland at this time of year. At any other time, Claire could not have failed to be stirred by it, today she barely noticed it. Her whole mind was centred on the one burning question. Was Rod having an affair with this woman? She had to be sure before she could even begin to think what she might do about it.

She didn't go to the dam itself, taking the fork before the cut and heading up the hill to bring the car to a standstill overlooking the scene of activity from a height of a couple of hundred feet or so. From here it was easy to pick out the site office because Rod's car was parked outside it. At least the pair of them had come straight back.

Too busy to come home but with time enough to make the trip into town with another woman. There had to be something in it. And how she was going to handle that knowledge, Claire couldn't even begin to think.

The question was decided for her when Rod rang through to the house at four, not long after she had got in.

'I'm leaving early,' he said. 'I thought we might go out for a meal by way of change.'

'Guilty conscience?' Claire asked bitingly, and put the receiver down with a trembling hand. She hadn't meant to say that, it had just come out. Yet having said it she was glad of it. Why let suspicion fester inside her? It was far better to have the whole thing out in the open. Better for them both.

Rod arrived home within the hour, coming into the house with his mouth set like a steel trap.

'What the hell was that about?' he demanded from the kitchen doorway. 'Am I supposed to know?'

'You should.' She didn't look up from the table where she was studiously arranging flowers in a stoneware vase. 'I hope you weren't thinking of taking *me* to the Copper Kettle too!'

There was a brief pause before he answered that one. 'All right, so you saw me in the Copper Kettle. I didn't see you, but that's beside the point. Why didn't you come over?'

'I'd have thought that was obvious,' she said. 'You were far too engrossed in your ... companion to welcome interruption. Especially from your wife!'

His laugh was short. 'Aren't you jumping to a few too many conclusions?'

'I don't think so.' She met his eyes without flinching. 'You were holding her hand.'

Dark brows lifted. 'You actually saw me do that?'

'No, but Dinah did.'

'Dinah!' The sound came out explosively. 'I should have known. Whenever that woman gets in on the act there's trouble!'

'She wasn't trying to cause trouble,' Claire denied. 'Are you saying it didn't happen?'

'Who would you rather believe?'

'You, of course.'

'All right then, it didn't happen.' Rod moved away from the doorway. 'Where would you like to go for dinner?'

Claire stared at him in some confusion. Did he really think that was all there was to it? She said hesitantly, 'You still haven't explained what you were doing in there with this Judy woman.'

'Eating,' he came back. 'It's what people tend to do in restaurants.'

'You know what I mean.'

He looked at her for a moment—an assessing look. 'I'm not going into any details,' he said. 'We happened to be in town together with a little time to spare, so I took her to lunch. That's all you need to know.'

Claire threw down the flowers she was holding, eyes blazing. 'I have a right to know! She works for you, doesn't she? She's the one you were so afraid of upsetting if I arrived on the scene.'

'True.' His calm was infuriating. 'She's efficient, attractive, and I wouldn't at all mind getting into bed with her, but so far it hasn't happened.'

'Meaning it might.'

'Meaning you'd better stop the damned catechism or something else will!' Sudden weariness showed in his eyes. 'It might not be a bad idea if you went to visit Bill for a few days, give you time to sort yourself out a little.'

'And you a free rein,' she retorted. 'You don't need to bother. I already thought of it. In fact, the sooner I can get away from this hole, the better!'

'Fine.' His face was expressionless now. 'Did you let him know?'

'Not yet.'

'Then there's no time like the present. We should catch him at the office. Do you want to tell him or shall I?'

'You do it.' She could barely get the words out. None of this had been intended—or at least, not this fast. She hoped suddenly that Bill would say no, she couldn't come to Meadowbank, as he had said to her the last time. She had the feeling that once she left Colwood she and Rod were through. And that wasn't what she wanted at all—was it?

Rod went out to the hall and dialled the STD code and number, waited a moment or two for the connection, and asked in a crisp voice to speak to Mr Naughton, giving his own name.

'Bill?' he said a moment later. 'Claire needs a break. Are you going to be in town for the next week or so if she comes down there?' He paused for the reply, his eyes on Claire's face through the open kitchen door. 'Yes, she's okay. Just not sure what she wants.' His mouth stretched briefly and without humour as the other voice spoke again. 'Not in this case. Expect her late afternoon. I'm not sure whether she'll be driving or coming by train. Whichever I suggest she'll do the other.' He held out the receiver to Claire. 'He wants to speak to you.'

It was the last thing Claire wanted, but there was no way out of it. She went through and took the instrument from him, steeling herself against the cool touch of his fingers. 'Hallo, Bill,' she said on a hollow note.

His voice came back gruffly, 'Claire, I've just one question to ask you. Are you sure you want to do this?'

She knew what he meant. He could recognise the finality too. She had her back to Rod so he couldn't see the stiffness about her mouth and jaw. When she spoke her voice sounded totally unemotional. 'Yes.'

'All right then, I'll see you tomorrow.' He was neither censorious nor sympathetic. 'Take care if you decide to bring the car.'

Claire put down the receiver carefully as the line went dead. She didn't want to look at Rod. He hadn't been able to wait to get rid of her.

And whose fault was that? she asked herself in sudden honesty. What support had she given him these last weeks? A long time ago she had told her father that the woman Rod married would have to be prepared to follow him wherever his job took him, and she had fallen at the first hurdle. Too late now for regrets. They had lost whatever they'd had.

Going out to dinner was obviously out of the question, considering. The meal Claire prepared turned out almost inedible because she couldn't keep her mind on what she was doing, but it hardly mattered as neither of them was in a mood to eat a great deal.

'What time are you thinking of leaving?' asked Rod over coffee.

'About ten, I suppose,' she said, not lifting her head. 'Unless you'd rather I took the train.'

'You'd have to set off at the crack of dawn to make the connection,' he pointed out. 'You'll make better time in the car once you hit the M1.'

'I wasn't sure you'd want me to take the car, that's all.'

His smile held cynicism. 'It's a bit late to start considering that angle. It's your car. You do as you like with it.'

The evening passed slowly with little more said between them. Claire packed a suitcase, hardly knowing what she put in it, then went downstairs again to make a bedtime drink for them both, remembering the times she had resented Rod's assumption that it was her job and hers alone. Heating milk, she wondered how he would react if she went through now and told him she had changed her mind about going away. Not that she had any real intentions. Emotionally she was ready to go—if a complete absence of feeling could be counted as ready.

She had thought of occupying the spare room again for the one night, but oddly enough when the time came she couldn't bring herself to do it. Lying in bed at Rod's side, she tried to consider the future, but all she saw was a blank wall. From tomorrow that was her life. And she had brought it on herself.

Rod was already up and in the bathroom when she awoke at seven-thirty. He was fully dressed apart from his tie when he came back into the bedroom. Choosing one from the wardrobe, he said. 'I'll be away by eight. I want to run a re-check before we blast at nine-thirty. Do you want some coffee bringing up?'

Claire shook her head, bringing the dark hair swinging forward to hide her face. In the light of morning, yesterday's suspicions seemed faintly ridiculous. If Dinah hadn't been with her matters would probably never have gone as far as they had, she acknowledged wryly. She might have felt moved to accuse Rod of neglect but not of having an affair with the woman on the strength of one meal together.

It still wasn't too late to admit her mistake and call off the trip south, she supposed—except that it was Rod himself who had proposed it first; she was forgetting that. Pride overrode the momentary weakness. She had to go. He didn't want her here.

'I'll make some fresh when I get down,' she said.

'Fair enough.' He looked at her across the width of the room, making no attempt to come over. 'I'll phone tonight after six to make sure you arrived okay. Take it easy on the motorway.'

He was gone before she could think of any reply. She doubted if there was an adequate one. His reasons for leaving early were simply an excuse, she decided dully. He would have checked and rechecked those figures long before this.

With her suitcase already packed there was little else to do but potter around once she was up. She could always leave early, of course, but something in her held back from that. Eleven would be soon enough.

The faint double rumble of the blast came while she was under the shower, causing a momentary drop in pressure. She was back in the bedroom and partially dressed when the telephone started ringing downstairs. Claire didn't answer immediately, thinking it might be Dinah, but it kept right on ringing until she was forced to go across and pick up the extension.

'Hallo?' she said tentatively.

The voice on the other end of the line sounded hoarse as if whoever was calling either had a very bad cold or was short of breath. 'Mrs Gilvray? Can you get out here to the site as soon as you can? I'm afraid there's been an accident.'

Fear swept through her like a bush fire. The blasting. Something had gone wrong with the blasting!

'You're saying my husband has been injured?' she said urgently. 'How badly?'

'I'm not sure.' The voice faded and came on again. 'Got to get back.'

'I'll be there in half an hour,' Claire told him before the line went dead. She let the receiver drop back into the rest with a crash and hastily pulled on the slacks and shirt laid ready, only pausing to snatch up her car keys from the dressing table where she had placed them last night in readiness. It was like that time with her father all over again, except that this time it was for real. It had to be serious if they had found it necessary to send for her directly like this. She found her lips moving in silent prayer as she flew downstairs.

That journey out to the dam was something she never remembered too clearly afterwards. Driving across the rolling purple moors, she was conscious only of the need to get where she was going in the shortest possible time. She had been such a fool. What did all her petty little grievances matter now? Rod was injured and she loved him. If she lost him she would die herself. She wouldn't want to live without him!

She was across the temporary bridge and screeching to a halt in front of the works office building downstream of the dam before she became aware of the odd lack of run-

ning confusion such as one might expect about the site
after any kind of major accident. So far as she could see,
work appeared to be progressing normally. It was all too
reminiscent of another time, another place. Realisation was
just beginning to crystallise in her mind when Rod came
out from the office.

He strode swiftly across to the car, pulling open the
door to view her white face with concern and not a little bewilderment. 'Claire, what is it? What's happened?'

Blinding relief mingled with mounting anger, the former
winning by a short head as she looked back at the man she
had visualised buried under a mountain of rubble.

'Bill,' she got out. 'It was Bill!'

'What was Bill?' His tone sharpened. 'Claire, *what* happened?'

'He said you'd been injured. Told me to get out to the
site as soon as possible.' She drew in a shaky breath, remembering what she had gone through this last half hour.
'That's twice he's done this to me! How could he? How
could he!'

'Move over,' Rod said quietly. 'We need somewhere
private to talk this out.'

She did so without argument, aware of curious eyes.
Speculation would be rife already. Not that she cared about
that. What she cared about was this man now sliding into
the seat she had just vacated and switching on the ignition.
He was all right. Compared with that nothing else really
counted.

He drove for a couple of miles before pulling the car to a
stop where the moorland road dipped to overlook the whole
dale below them. Claire watched the strong brown hands
apply the handbrake and switch off the engine, overwhelmed by the longing to feel them take hold of her.

'I'm not going away,' she said before he could speak. 'I
don't care whether you want me to or not, I'm not going!'

His smile warmed her. 'That sounds more like the girl I used to know. She never gave me any choice!'

'Oh, Rod,' her voice broke, 'I've been such an idiot! How can you still want me?'

'That's simple,' he said. 'I can't stop wanting you. I was going to give you just three days then come and get you —if I'd lasted that long.'

There was a sudden moist brightness about her eyes. 'Then Bill needn't have gone to all this trouble after all.'

'No, but I'm halfway glad he did. At least this way I'm assured you feel something about me.'

'*Something*?' Claire stared at him wonderingly. Surely it was as plain as the nose on her face how she felt! 'Rod, I *love* you! I know I haven't shown it so much these last few weeks, but it was there underneath all that selfishness.' She reddened a little remembering some of the things she had said and done, the total inconsideration she had shown. 'You were right, I was still just a spoiled brat. I wanted everything my own way.'

'That makes two of us,' he rejoined on a wry note. 'Pig-headed as they come! Only I should have known better. There has to be give and take from both sides, not just the one.' He studied her face for a long, revealing moment before reaching out to smooth away the tumbled hair from her eyes. 'You didn't even stop to put a comb through it, did you? That makes me feel very humble.'

'You couldn't feel humble if you tried,' she said, laughing through the sparkle of tears. 'And I wouldn't want you to. I love you the way you are—arrogant, domineering ...' She met his lips halfway, moulding herself to him with passionate abandonment, wanting him with everything in her because he was the only man for her.

They made love in the long cool grass beyond the dry stone wall, and it was like the first time again. Lying with her head cradled on his shoulder when it was over, Claire thought that nothing would ever compare with this moment for sheer unadulterated happiness.

'I never really believed you were having an affair with Judy Woods,' she said softly, wanting to have everything right. 'It was pure envy because you seemed to have more time for her than you gave to me.'

Rod was laughing; she could feel him doing it, although he didn't make any sound. 'What you're really saying is what the hell was I doing in that restaurant with her at all.'

'I am not——' she began, then stopped and started smiling herself. 'Well, all right, so I am. You have to admit, I had some cause to be jealous.'

'Every cause, on the face of it.' He rolled over on to his side, kissing her thoroughly and satisfyingly before going on. 'Her car was in the garage for testing and they'd have been closed by the time she could have got there after work. Having offered to run her in for it, I felt lunch was a perfectly understandable next step. Judy doesn't read too much into too little. Anyway, she's had enough of men as anything but friends or employers for the present.'

'How about the hand-holding?' asked Claire with tongue in cheek, and felt him lay his hand threateningly across her.

'Don't tempt me!'

'It's Dinah you should be doing that to, not me. She was the one who said it.'

'What I'd like to do to friend Dinah doesn't come under the heading of gentle chastisement,' he returned with feeling. 'A crop might be more appropriate! You're not seeing her again.'

'Are you asking me or telling me?'

'I'm telling you.'

She hid a smile. 'Then I won't of course.'

He looked at her for a long moment before his eyes started to crinkle. 'You learn fast.'

'Once I start,' she agreed. 'I meant it, though. I still

can't dislike Dinah, but I do think she's a bit of a trouble-maker.'

'Bored,' he suggested. 'Like someone else I know.' His expression underwent a change, the smile fading a little. 'It's going to be exactly the same as it was, you realise? For the next month or so at least. I could promise to try and spend more time at home, but it probably won't work out that way.'

'So I'll just have to occupy my time and my mind the best way I can,' said Claire without rancour. 'The way I'd have done from the first if I hadn't been so set on making you suffer.'

'You mean get a job?'

'Not if you're really so much against it.' She gave a mock sigh. 'You never heard of emancipation, did you?'

'Blame my father,' he came back lightly. 'Keep a woman in her place, he always said, and you'll have a life worth living. Let her out of it and she'll make it hell on earth! Maybe I deserve a little hell.'

'I'm not that eager to find a job,' Claire admitted softly. 'I'd rather have a baby. I know you said you wanted to wait, but you're almost thirty-three now. You don't want to be too old to enjoy your children, do you?'

There was a resigned tolerance in the curve of his lips. 'They'd better be boys or I don't stand a chance. Talking of fathers, we'd better contact yours and tell him you won't be joining him after all.'

'I imagine he has a good idea already. And I still haven't forgiven him. To play that trick once was bad enough, but *twice*! And I fell for it too!'

'I'm glad to say.' Rod shook his head, his eyes warm on her face. 'Don't knock my father-in-law. His methods might be a bit unorthodox, and he doesn't seem to have considered the chances of you meeting with an accident in the rush to get out here, but he brought us together again as nothing else might have done. For that I can only feel grateful.'

Me too, thought Claire, letting the last spark of resentment fade away as she bent to kiss her husband. She sent a silent message winging southwards: Thanks, Dad!

The Mills & Boon Rose is the Rose of Romance

Every month there are ten new titles to choose from — ten new stories about people falling in love, people you want to read about, people in exciting, far-away places. Choose Mills & Boon. It's your way of relaxing:

October's titles are:

NO PASSING FANCY by Kay Thorpe
Claire's father had tricked her into going out to Tanzania, and there she found herself thrown into the company of the forceful Rod Gilvray.

HEART OF STONE by Janet Dailey
'I live hard and fast and love the same way,' declared Brock Canfield. At least Stephanie knew where she stood — but was what he offered enough for her?

WIFE BY CONTRACT by Flora Kidd
Her marriage to Damien Nikerios had brought Teri money and position — and the humiliation of knowing that Damien had only married her as a cover-up for his affair with his father's wife.

WHEN LIGHTNING STRIKES by Jane Donnelly
Robina had an abiding detestation of Leo Morgan who was responsible for so much of her unhappiness. And yet her life seemed to be inextricably involved with him . . .

SHADOW OF DESIRE by Sara Craven
Ginny needed to keep Max Henrick at more than arm's length — which wasn't going to be easy when she was living and working in the same house.

FEAR OF LOVE by Carole Mortimer
If Alexandra wanted to marry Roger Young, that, she felt, was her own affair. Just what business was it of the high-handed Dominic Tempest?

WIFE FOR A YEAR by Roberta Leigh
Juliet had married Damon Masters to enable him to take an important job in one of the Gulf states. She had no feeling for him — or so she thought . . .

THE WINDS OF WINTER by Sandra Field
Anne Metcalfe had assumed a new name and identity to return, after four years, to her husband's house. She just *had* to discover if what she suspected was true . . .

FLAMINGO PARK by Margaret Way
What right did Nick Langford have to try and run Kendall's life for her? She was quite capable of looking after herself — wasn't she?

SWEET NOT ALWAYS by Karen van der Zee
Was Jacqueline's job in Ghana the real challenge, or was it Matt Simmons, her boss, who seemed so determined to think badly of her?

The Mills & Boon Rose is the Rose of Romance

Look for the Mills & Boon Rose next month

IMAGES OF LOVE by *Anne Mather*
Tobie couldn't resist seeing Robert Lang again, to exact her
revenge — but she didn't know what had happened to Robert
since they had last met . . .

BRAND OF POSSESSION by *Carole Mortimer*
Jake Weston's lack of trust in her ought to have killed all the
love Stacy felt for him — but it didn't.

DIFFICULT DECISION by *Janet Dailey*
Deborah knew that her job as secretary to the forceful Zane
Wilding would be difficult — but the real challenge was to her
emotions . . .

HANNAH by *Betty Neels*
Nurse Hannah Lang was happy to accompany the van Eysink's
back to Holland, but the unbending Doctor Valentijn van Bertes
was not quite so enthusiastic about it.

A SECRET AFFAIR by *Lilian Peake*
As a confidential secretary, Alicia was well aware how essential
it was to keep secret about her boss's new project. So why didn't
he trust her?

THE WILD MAN by *Margaret Rome*
Rebel soon realised how Luiz Manchete had earned his name —
the wild man — when she found herself alone with him in the
heart of his jungle kingdom . . .

STRANGER IN THE NIGHT by *Charlotte Lamb*
When Clare met Macey Janson, she began to lose some of her
fear of men. So why did Luke Murry have to turn up again,
making Macey suspect the worst of her?

RACE AGAINST LOVE by *Sally Wentworth*
Toni disliked Adam Yorke intensely, and her friend Carinna was
more than welcome to him! But did Toni *really* mean that?

DECEPTION by *Margaret Pargeter*
Sick to death of being run after for her money, Thea ran away
herself — but she only found a new set of problems . . .

FROZEN HEART by *Daphne Clair*
Joining an expedition to the Antarctic, Kerin was taken aback to
discover that the arrogant Dain Ransome was to be its leader . . .

If you have difficulty in obtaining any of these books from your
local paperback retailer, write to:

Mills & Boon Reader Service
P.O. Box 236, Thornton Road, Croydon, Surrey, CR9 3RU.

Available November 1980

Mills & Boon Classics

The very best of Mills & Boon
romances, brought back for those of you
who missed reading them when they
were first published.

In
October
we bring back the following four
great romantic titles.

NO QUARTER ASKED
by Janet Dailey

Stacy Adams was a rich girl who wanted to sample real life for
a change, so she courageously took herself off alone to Texas
for a while. It was obvious from the first that the arrogant
rancher Cord Harris, for some reason, disapproved of her — but
why should she care what he thought?

MIRANDA'S MARRIAGE
by Margery Hilton

Desperation forced Miranda to encamp for the night in Jason
Steele's office suite, but unfortunately he found her there, and
after the unholy wrath that resulted she never dreamed that a
few months later she would become his wife. For Jason was
reputed to be a rake where women were concerned. So what
chance of happiness had Miranda?

THE LIBRARY TREE
by Lilian Peake

Carolyn Lyle was the niece of a very influential man, and
nothing would convince her new boss, that iceberg Richard
Hindon, that she was nothing but a spoiled, pampered darling
who couldn't be got rid of fast enough! Had she even got time
to make him change his mind about her?

PALACE OF THE POMEGRANATE
by Violet Winspear

Life had not been an easy ride for Grace Wilde and she had
every reason to be distrustful of men. Then, in the Persian
desert, she fell into the hands of another man. Kharim Khan,
who was different from any other man she had met . . .

Doctor Nurse Romances

and October's
stories of romantic relationships behind the scenes
of modern medical life are:

SURGEON'S CHALLENGE
by Helen Upshall

Sister Claire Tyndall's success as a nurse was undoubted
— but as a woman? Richard Lynch and Dr Alan Jarvis
both made it clear that they were interested in her. Both
were handsome and determined, but both — unfortunately
for Claire — seemed to be married already!

ATTACHED TO DOCTOR MARCHMONT
by Juliet Shore

Doctor Sally Preston's relationship with her new chief,
Darien Marchmont, got off to a sticky start. So she was
less than pleased to discover that their first joint
assignment was a two-man medical survey in the heart
of the North African desert!

Masquerade
Historical Romances

Intrigue excitement romance

TARRISBROKE HALL
by Jasmine Cresswell

Utter ruin confronted the Earl of Tarrisbroke. Faced with discharging his father's mountainous gambling debts, what could he do but marry for money? But the wife he chose, the wealthy young widow Marianne Johnson, was not at all the vulgar title-hunting woman he expected!

ZULU SUNSET
by Christina Laffeaty

Cassandra Hudson wanted to be a missionary's wife — more particularly, her cousin Martin's wife. So she travelled to Zululand to visit him, confident that her new fortune would smooth her way. Unfortunately she found herself in the midst of an impending war between whites and Zulus, and the only man who could help her reach Martin was the odious, arrogant Saul Parnell ...

Look out for these titles in your local paperback shop from 10th October 1980